BEING HUMAN
Call of the Wild

BEING HUMAN
Call of the Wild

Edited By

GREGORY F. TAGUE

Editions Bibliotekos, Inc.

E♦B

New York

Editions Bibliotekos

Finding the Uncommon Reader

Fredericka A. Jacks, Publisher

Editorial Assistant: Meagan Meehan
Proofreader: Sharon Dittus

publisher@ebibliotekos.com
www.ebibliotekos.com

Printed & Bound in the United States

Set in Garamond

ISBN: 978-0-9824819-5-0

Editions Bibliotekos, Inc.
E♦B
New York

One's every action is inevitably conditioned by
one's surroundings and one's body.

–Tolstoy

CONTENTS

PREFACE

Gregory F. Tague & Fredericka A. Jacks

We are primarily interested in stories that deal with human character. Who are we as a species and as individuals? What is our human nature? While we have constructed, over thousands of years, a vast cathedral of scintillating, rational humanity, we can be primal and shadowy with visceral emotions. We can profoundly love and superficially hate. Though we are by nature social creatures, we can commit acts of aggression (either against ourselves or others). And yet, quite often, we seek through rituals a natural peace with ourselves in unison with our family or the larger environment.

What is our evolved human essence? What makes us tick as a species? At one point in history, as many as ten different hominid species roamed the planet, but only we endured. There is even speculation that seventy thousand years ago only a few thousand of our species were alive. Why *do* we struggle on, survive, build cathedrals (and yet hurt each other)? Why do we have rituals, and why do we create and sometimes destroy relationships? What is (in the phrase of one of our contributors) the human factor? What does it mean to be (simultaneously) a deeply meditative and a yet a spontaneously feeling human being?

The fact(or) of being human means recognizing that there is in each of us a call of the wild, however subtle. There is something elemental in us that lingers. Who hears the ancestral call? Who answers the call? What is the response of any individual to the *force* of being human? For most of our human history, we have not lived in cities but have developed from hunters and gatherers (roaming in small clusters) into engineers of sophisticated national languages and intricate cultures. How much of the old nature lingers in us still? Apparently quite a lot.

We are in a natural world from which we emerged; we are part of a large universe of nature; and we wrestle with aspects of our own human nature. Our history is such that we are social creatures who have evolved very complex emotions not only of sympathy and compassion, but also of jealousy and hatred. So the call of the wild does not mean running off into the woods and hunting fish with one's teeth; it means acknowledging our deeper connections to the earth beyond concrete buildings, and more importantly, our essential connection to each other.

There are aspects of our psyche (feelings and instincts) and of our physical structure (teeth and fingernails) with which we must reckon. While we have evolved superstructures of civilization, there are darker moments in our collective and individual histories, mostly (as this volume investigates) on a personal or inter-personal level. While familial creatures who create loving bonds, we are also capable of inflicting harm.

For this book we received quite a corpus of submissions – well over one thousand pages. We have tried to cull from that mass just enough material to make our literary point, but keep in mind that the stories between these covers consist of many different styles and voices. Much of the writing is poetic, magical, contemplative, and even humorous. We are sure that after having read this small book, you too will be captivated by the question, Who are we, individually and collectively?

FOREWORD

Ian S. Maloney

Being Human: Call of the Wild reminds readers of the varied, wonderful connections and tensions between the natural world and human civilization. There are many difficult questions posed in the book. Why do we kill certain creatures while nurturing others ("The Raccoon")? When do we draw the line between protecting our property and letting other creatures live and thrive ("Two Foxes")? What drives people to kill others to protect their land ("Through the Wagonwheel")? This anthology is about the beautiful mysteries surrounding us in nature. Wondrous images and ideas swirl and circulate through this book. Gold liquid from beehives flows onto the earth ("Four Liters of Wild Honey"). A granddaughter ("Potatoes") plants with her grandfather and contemplates the passing of life underground into "a formless mass of matter in which all was chaos and confusion." A miraculous migration of endangered butterflies is imagined to be the transfigured form of lost ancestors ("Annual Migration"). Many of these stories explore the lines cast under the surface of creation, characters looking for a nibble of understanding to make better sense of their place in an evolving world. Childhood memories collide with the progress of time and the varied human attempts to regulate and restrict nature, as seen in "White Kaleidoscope," "Suspended Lines" and "Writing on the Wall."

And yet, the precarious balance of harmony and chaos in the wild is met with human tenderness, hope, and courage.

We travel along with a spice merchant ("To Zanzibar") as he leaves the marketplace, his Tower of Babel, to encounter the far off places from where his spices originate. We wander away from mundane order into a magical Garden of Eden, where new cities and universes expand within the human soul through new interactions with minute particles and new people. We are drawn along through humor and pathos into the complexity of human existence, our persistent questions and confusions about our origins, our ultimate place in the universe. Comic interactions abound as we watch Ida Pilcher come to terms with her vultures (literally) in "Swirling Above Her Head" and another narrative voice invites us to hear her talking to a tree in the aptly titled "Conversation With a Tree."

Ultimately, this volume takes a turn from Jack London's pitting of nature against civilization; this is not a survival of the fittest, nature red-in-tooth-and-claw anthology. *Being Human* wonders in the mysterious, and often whimsical, play of humanity as it interacts with, and seeks solace and identification in, nature. In "The All-Knowing Eye," Garland Duckett finds God in the eyes of a Great Blue Heron. He moves beyond the strictures of his condo committee's regulations to find companionship with a woman creating a wildlife refuge in her backyard. Garland goes on a journey as we do in reading this volume. Nature continues to find a way to mystify and satisfy us, for it cannot be contained neatly, even as we try to box it off. As the stories testify, such exchanges aid us in our call of the wild to be more human, and thus to be more engaged with the world around us.

The Raccoon

Stephen Poleskie

Having discovered its presence from one of his upstairs windows, the no-longer-young man watches as a playful raccoon dances on the damp evening grass in his backyard. He is considering if this might be the same raccoon that has been lately raiding his bird feeder. On previous nights he has chased a raccoon away with loud noises and flashing lights, but now it's back. Or is it? This masked creature appears somewhat smaller and livelier than last night's visitor. Or is it a trick of the fading light on his fading vision?

Stealthily observing its gamesome movements, the man asks himself if raccoons aren't as equally entertaining as birds. He wonders why it is that he feeds the many birds that come to his backyard, buying them the most expensive sunflower seeds, while guarding these same seeds from squirrels and raccoons in a special feeder, with a spring loaded lid that closes whenever anything heavier than a blue jay steps on the feeding rail. The thing is mounted high up on a pole girdled by a tin baffle that does keep squirrels away, but only serves as a buffet stand for the crafty raccoons.

Without a sound the raccoon moves closer to the house, and the man's bounteous bird feeder. A butterfly flutters by in the twilight, the sun's last rays slanting off its black and golden wings. Through the slightly open window he hears the whir of

1

a hummingbird, but the tiny flyer is quickly gone before his searching eyes can find it.

Darkness is rapidly gathering itself around the well-ordered acre that makes up the man's backyard, all that separates his world from the wild extravagance of the woods beyond. He can still see clearly enough to recognize that it is a young raccoon that is coming, with its strange pavane, moving stealthily into his domain. He wants to tell the raccoon that it has come too early. This creature has not yet learned that its kind ply their trade at night: knocking over his garbage cans and scattering the contents, robbing his bird feeder, digging up his wife's plantings to look for grubs. Or would this raccoon tell the man that it was its rival the skunk that committed these crimes against his space – this land that he bought forty years ago, as a young man, so he would not have the bother of neighbors, and on which he currently pays such high property taxes that the now old man spends almost as much money per year in taxes as he originally paid to buy the land.

The moon has already appeared although the sun is only half hidden behind the trees. If his wife were home this evening, not gone to visit her ailing mother, the man would not be looking out the window scouting his backyard for intruders, but sitting on the couch, watching old movies on television with her, which they usually did after dinner, sometimes seeing the same film for the third or fourth time.

The raccoon has risen up on its hind legs, head held high sniffing the wind, its masked face looking, as his wife would say, "adorable." Its eyes are studying the man's bird feeder – as if deciding if this is where it will dine this evening. Upstairs, lying with his belly pressed to the squeaky bed, the man slowly eases the barrel of his shotgun out the open window. He is careful not to make any noise. His enemy, wandering about randomly, disappears under the garden bench. All the man can do is wait.

Scampering back out into the open, crossing the grass on all fours, the raccoon is in the man's sight, the setting sun reflecting in the fluorescent plastic insert at the end of the two barrels. The marauder, its form obscured by the glowing plastic, is no longer a living creature, only a blurred, gray target. The man's thumb inches the safety lock forward. Perhaps the raccoon hears this, or perhaps it is intuition – the creature starts to run. The man squeezes the trigger, not carefully as he has been taught to do, but hurriedly, jerking the gun upward. The right barrel sends out its expanding circle of deadly pellets, each one seeking flesh – the single purpose that they have been designed to fulfill.

One, or perhaps more, of the tiny, metal balls must have hit its mark. The raccoon falls, rolls over, and then gets up again and runs for the garden. It crashes down, crawling into the safety of the tomato plants. Hidden from the man's view, the raccoon begins the pitiful cry of a wounded animal. It needs another hit to stop the misery but is just beyond the edge of the house – the man cannot get a clear angle for his shot.

Without thinking, the man rushes down the stairs, plunging into darkness, forgetting to turn on the lights in his haste, forgetting that he is old and has fallen on these same stairs several times in the past, forgetting that he is carrying a shotgun with one barrel still loaded, and the safety left in the "fire" position.

The three family cats, roused from their sleep by the noise of the shot, scurry about the kitchen, crowding under the man's feet, racing him to the door. "Go away cats! Get back, stay in the house!"

He cannot let them out, their beloved cats – there is a dying animal, not much bigger than they are, out there in the darkness. Despite the cats' instincts, the man had tried to teach them not to kill. He took away baby rabbits and squirrels they caught, even nursing back to health a particularly pitiful squirrel that one of them had brought to him when the cat tired of playing with it since it was so near death, and no longer entertaining. The cat had not killed it, but brought it to him, and he had saved it, feeding it birdseed from his hand. How could he feed a dying squirrel from his hand and yet shoot other squirrels and raccoons who would take the same seeds from the feeder on their own?

The man stands at the edge of his garden, in the dark shadows, his body shaking, pointing the barrels of his shotgun at the whimpering sounds of dying. He slides the safety back and squeezes the trigger. There is no response. Confused, he squeezes the trigger again. Then he realizes that the safety has been off all the while, and he has unconsciously moved it to on. Moving the safety to the fire position, the man aims the ready gun into the darkness, in the direction that the pitiful sound has been coming from.

But he can hear no noise, only silence, an echo of the tremulous creature's despair, as the raccoon is alive no more. The man feels a tightness growing in his throat. A pale shaft of light momentarily wafts down from the yellow distance and is gone. The garden becomes black and brittle, as if has disintegrated into one, enormous emptiness.

And then suddenly there are two lights behind him – coming closer. The man turns around. He aims his gun at the bright intruder, and then instantly points it down. It is his wife's car pulling into the driveway. She has returned from visiting her mother who is in the hospital. She does not approve of him killing anything, even creatures that rob the tomatoes from the plants that she has so carefully tended.

"It was a raccoon . . . I just fired the gun to scare it away . . . it ran off into the bushes," the man lies.

There is an electronic click as his wife locks the car doors. In the darkness he cannot see the expression on her face.

"And how is your mother doing?"

She does not answer but takes his hand and slowly leads her husband into the house.

~

The proudest animal that nature produces respects its own form in another. Humankind is the only animal that preys on its own kind. — Boileau

Two Foxes

Arthur Powers

(Tocantins – Brazil, 1991)

"Foxes," Adão said.

It was six in the morning. October, a cool day at the beginning of the rainy season. The two foxes stood outlined against the gray morning sky on the dirt road ahead of us. Brazilian foxes: slightly larger than a North American fox, brownish gray, sturdy, with great bushy tails. I slowed the jeep. The lead fox darted ahead into the tall grass at the right side of the road. The other hesitated a moment, then turned and vanished off to the left.

"Foxes," he said again. His big black face peered across me into the bush on the left, to see if he could spot the one that had run there. Then a deep, loving laugh rolled out from his big body.

"You have many of them out at your farm?" I asked.

"Quite a few."

"They go after the chickens?"

"They sure do."

The jeep bumped along another half mile. I thought of that deep, rolling laugh. It was not the usual response to foxes.

"Most of the time, when there's someone in the car with me and we see a fox, they tell me to run it down." I shifted into second and maneuvered around a mud hole. "I never do, though."

We rode along in silence for a while. I glanced over at him – his gray hair and mustache, his big work-hardened hands, the new blue shirt and recently pressed gray pants he had worn into town.

"They almost always travel in couples like that, don't they?" I asked.

He smiled – a big, slow smile.

"I was just thinking of that," he said. "It reminded me of something that happened a few years ago."

"What was that?"

Adão didn't answer right away. I was thinking of his farm, where we were now headed. How you come to it over a slight rise. It lies in a green valley, looking like a farmstead might have looked any time in the last hundred years – the adobe house and outbuildings with palm-leaf thatched roofs, the wooden split-rail fences. He lives there with his daughter, his son-in-law, and their three children.

"It was a year or so after Adela died," he said. Adela was his wife. "A couple of hours before dawn. I was lying in my hammock, awake – staring at the dark, not wanting to get up and stir around so as not to wake the others. Suddenly I heard barking and growling – almost like a dog fight. I rolled out of the hammock, put on my boots, grabbed my flashlight and rifle, and headed out the door.

"It was a moonlit night. We had three dogs then, and I saw them over by the fence. They had something cornered. We'd been having trouble with foxes – so I guessed that's what it was. You know – when you farm like we do, you don't have much. Losing chickens hurts – and I was mad as hell. I raised my rifle and called off the dogs so that I could get a clear shot.

The dogs backed off – I shot and saw the fox leap up once and fall. I walked over – it was a big male, and he was dead – shot clean through the body. I started to turn back toward the house.

"Suddenly I glimpsed a rapid shadow scurrying from the end of the fence toward the woods. I wheeled, raised my rifle and shot. I heard a yip – but she kept running. It was a she-fox I was sure – smaller than the dead male. I fired again, but she was already into the woods and gone.

"The dogs went wild and started to chase her – but I called them off and walked toward the house. Everybody was awake now, of course, the grandkids rolling wide-eyed out the door wanting to see what had happened. So we took care of the dead fox, and talked, and my son-in-law and I told the kids all the fox stories we knew – and then some – and my daughter made us all a big breakfast. And that was that."

He went into one of his long pauses as I downshifted and headed up a winding, rutted slope. I waited.

"Except, well . . . I couldn't get it out of my mind. It kept eating at me. So, along about mid-morning, I took my rifle and the oldest dog, and I started out toward the woods.

"I'd hit her, all right. It was easy enough to see that. There was blood where I'd hit her, and blood here and there on the brush along the trail. That old dog and I had done our share of tracking, and it was easy enough to follow where she went. We curved off way to the southeast, until we came to a place where she seemed to have settled down for a while. Then the trail headed straight north.

"Now I'm no expert on foxes – or on anything else, for that matter – but there was only one reason I could think of for her doing that. As it turned out, I was right.

9

"Well, we headed north along her trail. The dog I brought with me was an old fellow – old enough to have some sense." He smiled at me. "Dogs are a lot like people in that way. Anyhow, he knew how to go quietly and not get over excited, keep his nose down and do his work. More than you can say for some folks."

He chuckled – a deep sound from down inside – then sat quietly a few seconds before continuing.

"When you've been in and out of the woods as long as I have, you get a sense for things. We reached a spot where I had that sense. I told the dog to lie down and be still. I moved forward, silently – slowly, pausing every few seconds. It wasn't close – it took me maybe half an hour to go a hundred yards. There was a small rock hill in front of me, with a cover of bush. Her trail – dim but still visible – led up to it. I moved slowly, quietly, raised my rifle with my right arm and pushed the branches aside quickly with my left.

"There she was. Not ten feet away – her teeth bared and her eyes on my eyes. My bullet that morning had hit her right shoulder – grazed deeply. The wound was still open, bleeding a little. She had lost blood – probably lost some mobility – and was tired. But that's not why she didn't run from me now. Behind her were three pups."

We had reached the final turn off to his farm. I slowed the jeep to navigate the narrower road.

"I want to explain how it was," he said. "A man has a right to defend what is his. A man has to feed his family – to fight off anything that steals from the mouths of his grandchildren. A man has a right to kill a fox."

He was silent for a moment.

"But a man also has a right – sometimes – not to kill."

We came over the last rise. The farm lay below us, beautiful and peaceful in the morning light.

"Here we are – home!" His voice was filled with contentment.

"Wait a minute!" I said, as I steered the jeep down the final slope. "What happened? What did you do?"

"What do you think I did?" he asked, laughing heartily.

"And you still have trouble with foxes?"

"Sure do. Probably the pups I left her to raise. That's gratitude for you, huh?" And he smiled.

■

Four Liters of Wild Honey

(Tocantins – Brazil, 1991)

Shatter. Crack.

João heard the bottle shatter an instant before the gunshot. Heard it and felt it. In his own slow way, he looked up to where the four clear-glass bottles of honey had stood, on a wooden railing, golden in the sunlight. Stood where they caught sunlight and the eyes of drivers on the Belém-Brasília highway – drivers who might stop and buy at his sister Marilda's roadside stand.

Shatter. Crack.

Another bottle shattered to the ground, bleeding gold honey into the roadside gravel. João's slow middle-aged body started forward with uncharacteristic speed, his mind focused on saving the remaining two bottles. But even as he got there

– shatter, crack – he felt the swish of the bullet and a third bottle shattered to the ground. He grabbed the fourth and pulled it close to his body – a slow motion goalie retrieving a rebound.

"*Idiota!*"

He turned and looked at the pickup truck, at the big florid man leaning on the open passenger door, pistol in hand. It was a new shining-white double-cabined truck with a chrome, shark toothed grill – bright even despite road dust. The truck was perhaps 50 feet away, pulled up at the other end of the stand. Beyond it, the empty two-lane highway stretched north across the dry, flat savannah land.

Marilda and the driver of the pickup – bills in hand ready to pay for fresh corn – stood frozen and staring at the man. Then they moved quickly.

"What is this?" Marilda shouted angrily as the driver started toward the truck, toward the man with the pistol. "Luiz!" the driver shouted.

The big florid man turned to the other.

"Tell that idiot to get out of the way," he complained. He was drunk. The driver reached him, spoke to him quietly, urgently. Luiz seemed to lose interest, allowing the driver to take the pistol out of his hand and coax him back into the truck.

"What is this?" Marilda shouted again, her sharp voice piercing the air.

The driver turned back to her. "I'm sorry, my brother . . ."

"That's wild honey," she said. "Fifteen *cruzados* . . ." João looked up startled. Normally they sold them for nine.

". . . and we have to clean up this mess."

Embarrassed, the driver was reaching in his wallet, pulling

12

out a fifty note, then another twenty. "Here," he said. And then again, confused, "I'm sorry . . ."

He picked up his sack of corn, put it in the back of the truck, walked around to the driver's door and got in. The door banged shut – strong metal – the engine revved up, the truck pulled out into the highway and headed south toward Goiania.

João eased down onto his three legged leather stool. He was still holding the fourth bottle. Marilda walked over to him. She was counting the money.

"You all right?" she asked.

He slowly nodded.

She was quiet for a moment, looking at the three shattered bottles, the gold honey – bright with splintered glass – flowing out onto the gravel.

"We made a lot more than we would have," she said.

He nodded again.

He sat on his three legged stool. He could sit there for hours – watching, thinking. "Let me handle the money," Marilda had always said. He knew how to count it, how to make change. But she was right – it didn't mean anything to him.

He looked again at the shattered bottles lying on the ground. Did *she* understand? Going out beyond the field, into the savannah backland – the wind-twisted trees, the low growing ground palms, the endless grass. You saw the bees and followed them, finding the hive. You gathered dried leaves and twigs and *lenha* – small limbs of dry, twisted wood. Carefully you placed them, preparing them with knowing hands. You had to do it just right to make smoke, enough smoke. You lit the fire, then walked away and stood back, watching – watching the smoke slowly rise and grow thicker, until the bees began to leave the hive – then their movement, a few at first going off and suddenly the whole swarm rising and flying away.

Then the hive itself. The careful handling of the rich white-yellow honey combs. Later, at home, filtering the golden liquid into the clear bottles. Thinking (with pictures, not with words) – this will bring memory to the lips of old people, now living in the city – memory of the countryside where they were young; this will bring happiness to children – eating quickly and licking with swift tongues; this will bring sweetness to men and women who rush, burdened, through their days.

His eyes caressed the shattered bottles, the shards of glass, the gold flowing into the ground. Slowly he rose and walked over to the wooden railing, and placed the last remaining bottle where it caught the bright afternoon sun.

A big Mercedes truck whirred by, raising a brief breeze. The noise of its motor grew fainter and fainter as it moved north. The silence of the savannah remained. Off to the west he heard the cry of the timid ground bird – *inhambu chororó* – calling out its notes in a descending scale.

Potatoes

Lisa M. Sita

In the late afternoon sunshine of September, Olivia knelt in the soil of her grandfather's garden, a lush, fertile secret hidden behind the busy streets of Brooklyn. Most of it grew in wild profusion, a tangle of flowers and bushes and old fruit-bearing trees that each year offered stunted apples, tart pears, and yellow cherries to the neighborhood's birds and squirrels. But on one side, against the high wooden fence that separated their yard from the neighbors', a wide strip of earth had been cleared for growing vegetables.

Trowel in hand, Olivia could hear her grandmother's voice carrying through the screen of the window above the sink calling to Olivia's sister in another room. Olivia's sister was older, married, with a baby on the way. The inviting smell of a roast wafted across the yard. Dinner would be ready soon.

She carefully pressed the tip of the trowel into the soil, lifted the dirt, went a little deeper, tentatively, searchingly, until a small brown knot the size of an elongated ping pong ball emerged. Olivia picked it up, sifted the dust off, and recognized the form of a potato – a miniature one, complete with tiny bumps and ridges on its rough brown surface. She returned the trowel to the soil and unearthed more potatoes, all of them miniscule, toy-like. She had misjudged. She had dug them up too soon.

They had planted the potatoes in March, she and her grandfather, a month before her eleventh birthday. She remembered how he had prepared a place for the potatoes in the moist earth, carefully loosening the soil and telling stories while he worked, as he often did, of the time when gods and goddesses entangled themselves in the affairs of the mortal world. Olivia helped by removing stray stones and pebbles while her grandfather passed on the story of creation as Ovid had passed it on to the people of Rome millennia ago.

All of nature had been one, her grandfather explained, a lumpy bundle of everything that existed, without shape or order – a formless mass of matter in which all was chaos and confusion. The land and air and oceans, all the planets and stars, the earth and sun and moon – everything trapped inside a single body, forever at war. Heat fought with cold, wet with dry, hard things with soft, until some entity – God or Nature – settled the disputes by liberating one from the other so that the sky was separated from the earth, the water from land, and the world, altered as it was, could evolve out of the mayhem it had been. Everything was then free to find its place – the fish were given water to live in, the birds air, the four-legged animals the earth to run upon and make their home. But something was missing, something different, and so people were born, the only creatures that could stand erect and lift their faces to heaven.

"So you see," her grandfather concluded, "that's why everything has its place."

Olivia thought for a moment.

"It sounds a lot like the Bible story," she said.

He nodded.

"I wonder how it happened for real. And when. How and when we all came to be."

"Who knows?" Her grandfather got up from the ground,

the knees of his dark green work pants brown with earth stains. "It doesn't really matter, does it? Everything has its place, and that's what's important."

From what she could figure, Olivia had to agree with him. There did seem to be a place for everything, a natural, unchanging order that could be counted on to endure – the animals and rocks, the forests and deserts, the flow of rivers and the stillness of the night sky – even the life of their family, three generations living contentedly together in one big, comfortable house. And now these potatoes, in their bed by the garden fence, growing slowly, silently, deep in the dark soil.

Each year for as long as she could remember, Olivia had watched her grandfather planting in the garden – the tomatoes, the basil and oregano, the peppers – had helped to turn the earth or just watched as he expertly tended the plants into maturity. She often would check the progress of the tomatoes, watch the small, green knobs ripen into juicy red fruit hanging heavily on the vines. She would keep a vigil over the even surface of the soil, waiting for the slender stems of the young plants to break through so that she could be witness to their growth and the nurturing power of the sun and her grandfather's vigilant watering. But she and her grandfather had never planted potatoes before. This time they were doing something new, untried, an experiment in cultivation. There would be no way for her to monitor the life of the potatoes underground. Their evolution would be a mystery to her, a present to be opened when the time was right, and only her grandfather would be able to say when that would be.

"That's it," he said, after running the hose on the soil to

water the potatoes. "We're finished."

She swirled the toe of her sneaker in the little rivulets of mud the water had made.

"What are you doing?" he said gruffly. "You're making a mess." He often sounded gruff. It was the way his words came out.

"I'm not doing anything," she said, continuing to swirl. She liked the way the muddy water made patterns as it drained off the rubber tip of her sneaker.

Her grandfather shook his head and walked away.

She saw him again at dinner, when he sat as he usually did, stoic and straight, a large glass of wine by his plate, and then later in the night, when it was time to go to bed. He was sitting in his favorite room at the front of the house in his easy chair by the long windows, watching television. On the screen in the corner, across from where he sat, a lion stalked gracefully through a golden grassland. The narrator's voice was deep and confidential. Olivia's grandfather leaned back in his chair, his head heavy against the green vinyl. He was open-mouthed, closed-eyed, snoring. The wall directly in front of him was shelved with Book-of-the-Month Club selections, rows of National Geographic magazines, and a few of her grandmother's knick-knacks scattered about.

Olivia walked into the room to say good-night. Her grandfather opened his eyes and leaned sleepily into her kiss as her lips brushed the soft lines of his cheek. His hair was silver and thin, brushed back from his forehead. As she was leaving, she glanced at his books and magazines. She noticed that the lion on the television had just leapt down from a magnificent rock, and in the background the African sky was the color of a bonfire. There were worlds in that room.

Numberless kinds of people, a planet of changing continents and exotic wildlife began there.

She did not know at the time that he had been sick; the adults had kept it from her. It was an enlarged heart, she learned later, one that could no longer work properly. Olivia knew only that for a long time he had to take it easy, could not eat certain foods, was told to eliminate from his diet the large glass of wine he always poured at dinner, and this she only knew from her mother and grandmother reprimanding him for violating some doctor's order or another. He did not listen to them. He enjoyed his small pleasures – his wine, his favorite foods. His heart was bad, he knew; changing the habits of a lifetime would not cure him. He was sixty-seven years old.

Before his death that July, he had predicted the birth of the baby Olivia's sister was carrying.

"August thirtieth," he said.

Olivia's sister disagreed: "The doctor says mid-September."

"No," he said, "August thirtieth."

He had been a witness to their courtship, Olivia's sister and her fiancé, when they would stay up late in her grandmother's kitchen and he would wander in from his front room to get a glass of water.

"Don't you think it's getting late?" he would say.

That was the signal for the evening to end; good girls did not stay up all night with their young men.

By the time her sister was married, their grandfather's illness had begun. The photos of him at the wedding showed a pale, drawn face, a tired smile hiding the inner war that was being waged inside his body.

When he had first entered the hospital Olivia went to visit

him, and he was pleased that she, a child, had come to such a stark, sterile place to see him. She did not think there was any significance to the illusion that he somehow looked smaller to her in the hospital gown – smaller and drained – not the tall, strong man they knew at home. His arm hung with loose skin as he lifted it to offer a hug when she left, but that did not deter her from believing he would be okay. He would regain his strength, she knew. He needed this rest so that the doctors could heal him. She kissed the top of his forehead. It was the last time she saw him.

The call from the hospital came one bitterly hot evening a few days later, as Olivia was sitting in the upstairs living room with her father and grandmother. Olivia could hear her mother's voice on the phone in the hallway, the sound of the receiver hitting its cradle as she hung up. A few moments later her mother was standing in the entranceway, limply leaning against the doorjamb. At the sight of her, Olivia's grandmother crumpled into a chair. Her father, his face chiseled with grief, got up and went to them. Olivia felt a cavernous emptiness beginning to open up inside her. She was lost, caught between the hollowness of herself and the force of the raw pain before her eyes. What was this thing that had happened to them, this sudden, violent wrenching of their lives?

In the days that followed, she watched the adults solemnly stumble through their days, making funeral arrangements, talking teary-eyed into the phone when friends and family called. One day, visitors she had never seen before showed up at their house. They wore dark clothes and frowns of empathy as they shook their heads and spoke in low tones to her mother and grandmother.

She did not attend the wake or the funeral. She was told not to. To see him like that, the body without the man, would have been too difficult, they felt, and so she remained home with relatives, unwilling to think of him resting in a coffin, soon to be lowered into the soft, moist earth.

It was not until later, in their dull, stupefied grief that her mother pointed out an oddity: while the electricity remained on, the kitchen clock plugged into the wall had stopped at the time of her grandfather's death. They took it as a sign: he was with them still and always would be. Yet it did little to still their pain. Nothing could distract their attention until the following month when Olivia's sister delivered the baby to lighten their mourning. The child, a girl, was born on the thirtieth of August.

Now, a month after the birth, Olivia was carrying back to the house in a brown paper lunch bag the tiny potatoes over which she and her grandfather had labored six months earlier.

"They're too small," she said to her mother, who was setting the table, and to her grandmother, who was busy at the stove. They both turned to look as Olivia pulled out one of the potatoes and held it up. She called to her sister in the front room to come and take a look.

"How cute," her sister said, looking at the tiny growth in Olivia's outstretched hand. Olivia could feel the frown of disappointment on her face.

"Cute?"

Her mother smiled. "It's okay," she said. "Sometimes when a vegetable is small it has a sweeter taste."

Her grandmother asked, "How do you want to eat them?"

"French fries," she said. "Tiny little French fries."

She got to work on peeling the skins while her grandmother

pulled out a small frying pan from one of the cabinets. Olivia covered the bottom of the pan with a layer of olive oil, turned on the gas, then neatly sliced the potatoes over the stove, letting the thin pieces fall directly onto the oil. This was the closest she had ever come to cooking. She did not like the idea of cooking, but there she was, frying potatoes, and not minding at all.

As the French fries sizzled to a crispy golden color, her father came into the kitchen, followed by her sister and brother-in-law. The table was set, with spaces left for the steaming platters of meat and fresh vegetables that her grandmother would place before them. The baby was in her bassinette by the window, Olivia soon took her place at the table, and that evening they all tasted the fruit of the potato harvest in honor of her grandfather. Olivia's mother was right; in their smallness, the potatoes were sweet.

Swirling Above Her Head

Andrea Vojtko

Ida Pilcher peered out the storefront window of Lou's TV Repair shop anxious about the vulture she spotted high in the sky. Blinded by the late September sun, she looked down and caught her reflected image in the grimy plate glass, causing her to frown. Her middle-aged face was puffy and beginning to take the shape of a potato, as was her short squat body.

Floyd Beasley pulled his van into Lou's parking lot in front of the store and Ida went over to the shelf on the far wall to get his still-broken nine-year old TV. With an audible grunt, she hoisted the 25-inch set onto the counter.

"Did you fix it?" Floyd asked entering the shop.

"Look here, Floyd, your cats peed in this TV and they shorted all the connections," she said elevating her monotone voice. "Our warranty doesn't cover cat pee. See. It says right here." She pointed to a clause in fine print.

"What are you talking about? That's a lot of crap," he shouted pushing away the warranty papers she held out to him.

"Floyd, you can just leave and take your TV with you. I'm not taking that kind of stuff," Ida said.

"What good's a warranty if you have an excuse for everything?" he ranted. "Good for nothing," he mumbled.

"What did you say?"

"I said you're good for nothing," he blurted.

"Just leave here, Floyd. I don't have to take that."

Floyd picked up his TV, grumbling, and banged the door on his way out.

Ida didn't like Floyd saying she was good for nothing. Everybody in Hobbs knew she was a hard worker, not only at Lou's but when she worked at Nelson's Hardware store and before that at the Cozy Diner. She couldn't help what the warranty read.

"His cables!" She grabbed them from the counter and rushed outside to catch him before he left. She didn't like leaving the shop because of the vulture problem. It made her nervous. For the past two weeks about a dozen turkey vultures swirled in a vortex fifty feet above her head every time she went outside. Then they followed her or her Chevy 4x4 pickup all around town. It was peculiar and she was afraid to mention it to anyone.

As she approached Floyd's van with the cables, she caught sight of some vultures descending in the sky above her.

"What did you bring those buzzards with you for?" he smirked, following her gaze upward. She turned and walked back to the shop.

It was time to close up shop, but she waited another half hour hoping the vultures would fly away. Finally she put on her bulky West Virginia Mountaineers jacket to leave, opened the door slowly, and made a break for the beat-up Chevy truck that she always parked on the far end of the lot. Like evil omens, ten or twelve vultures swooped over the roof from behind the shop and caught up with her just as she got to her truck. They were about as high as the four-story building next door, and their scary six-foot wingspan was tilted slightly upward in a V-shape. Their bald, red turkey heads looked down at her, making her feel nauseous as they spiraled above her head, descending and rising, descending and rising.

What the dang was going on? Vultures were only supposed to go after road-kill and dead things. She wondered if they smelled something in her that wasn't quite right and imagined a large decaying growth somewhere in her body. Stop thinking about things that aren't real, she told herself. As she headed home, she looked back at an outside mirror she had tilted upward on the back of her truck and saw the vultures still following her.

Looking at her watch, she turned her thoughts back to her family. She decided to stop at the Burger Boy to get take-out for supper.

"Four Burger Boy's and four large fries," she said into the microphone at the drive-through.

"Do you want the meal?" a foreign voice asked.

"No. No soda," she answered. She wasn't paying for extras.

At the pickup window a middle-aged Indian woman with a red dot on her forehead and a broad smile handed her a bag of burgers and fries. Ida noticed her nameplate read, "Shanti." She gave her a twenty and waited for her change. After a long minute, Shanti handed her the change and in a sing-song tone chimed, "Have a beautiful evening." Ida was too busy counting the coins to respond. Once she was short-changed by a foreigner that worked at the Burger Boy and she wasn't going to let that happen again.

Ida twisted back to look into her tilted mirror and noticed the vultures were still there. When she turned forward, Shanti was leaning out the window watching her. Ida's husband, Duanne, and her two boys, Ernie and Frankie, were the only ones who knew about the vultures before Floyd saw them.

Now this Indian lady knows, she thought.

When Ida got to her farmhouse two miles outside town she left the burgers, fries and a pitcher of lemonade on the kitchen table and told her sons to dig in. She took a few beers and burgers and went over to Duanne's hubcap shop next to the house. The shop was a two-story white cinderblock building like a small warehouse. The lower floor had a wall-sized window decorated with all kinds of hubcaps arranged around the edge. Every ornate and modern variation of swirling chrome spokes and sculpted air holes decorated the hubcaps. Some had four or five thick lug nuts in the center; others had smooth centers with some flattened like a Frisbee and others elevated like a dome. From the road they looked like elaborately-designed silver buttons. Stenciled in the middle of the window in faded red letters were the words "Hubcap Heaven."

"I got take-out today, Duanne; I was running late," she said as she lumbered into the store. Shelves and crates of old hubcaps, some sparkling and some grimy, overwhelmed the interior.

"How come you're running late?" Duanne's attention was riveted on the spokes of a hubcap he was polishing. He was six feet tall, lanky, and still good-looking with his little moustache and wavy black hair.

"Them vultures are still following me around," Ida answered.

"Yeh? That's the weirdest thing," he said, stopping his work to plunge into the burgers and beer that Ida dropped on the counter. She pulled up a stool and joined him.

"They really have it out for you for some reason, Ida," Duanne said.

"What did I do?" Ida asked.

"Not a damn thing," he answered, engrossed in his meal. He and Ida got married when they were both twenty-two and Ida discovered she was pregnant. At first Duanne worked in the coal mines, but he squirreled away enough money to build the hubcap shop he had always dreamed about.

"Well, then why are they after me?" The vultures conjured up scary things, a freak of nature or something weird or supernatural. Ida didn't know too much about nature, even though she'd lived all her life surrounded by mountains and wildlife in West Virginia. Nor was she religious. Yes, sometimes she took her two boys, Ernie and Frankie, to the Church of the Assembly, but that was just to teach them some guilt feelings so they didn't think they could do just anything they wanted.

"I don't know why they're following you. Anything unusual happen at Lou's lately?" Duanne mumbled, chewing his food.

"No. Just the same old things. Floyd Beasley got bent out of shape today when we wouldn't fix his TV. He started sassing me," she said. "But you know me, Duanne; I just told him to take his business someplace else if he was going to cuss at me like that. I had to take some cables out to his van and them vultures were out there and he saw them and made fun of me."

"You want me to go and bust his chops?" Duanne asked, playfully jabbing her arm.

"No. Don't do anything like that," she said. "Them vultures have been following me for about two weeks now. They just started following me for no reason I can figure."

"Don't worry about it. They'll go away sooner or later," he tried to reassure her.

~

The next evening Ida decided to make a country supper for her family to make up for the fast food the night before. She carried a baked ham with pineapple rings, brown sugar and cloves to the table and then some candied sweet potatoes. Finally, she brought over a plate of steaming corn on the cob. The comforting smell of home cooking filled the farmhouse.

"Frankie, Ernie, supper's ready," she yelled through the opened kitchen window. They were playing catch in front of the hubcap shop.

Duanne was sitting at the table reading the classifieds in the evening edition of the Hobbs Gazette looking for hubcap deals. Sometimes he had to travel to car junkyards or shows to get supplies, but a lot of people came to him with their old hubcaps, and he had a reputation for giving them a fair price for something like a 60's Ford spinner or a Cadillac wire spoke. If he wasn't around, Ida knew enough to tell a good hubcap from a dud.

Frankie and Ernie came in, slumped into their chairs at the table and reached for the food Ida had prepared. Frankie was eleven; Ernie was a senior in high school.

"Hey, partner," Duanne said pushing Ernie playfully in his thin shoulders. "You know, I've been thinking, Ida, why don't we send this guy to college next year? Get us a college graduate in the family."

Ida concentrated on cutting up the ham on her plate and didn't answer immediately. "You know what I think about college, Duanne," she said finally, like the issue was settled a long time ago.

"I wanna be a writer or a reporter for CNN," Ernie said enthusiastically.

Ida looked at Ernie, "A writer? What kind of money are you going to make being a writer? You think CNN is going to have a reporter in West Virginia?"

Ida chewed her food looking off in the distance. "What you want to do is get a job on that new bypass highway, driving heavy equipment. There's where the money is. There's something you can count on giving you a good living."

"Ernie's not big enough for construction, Ida. Look at him," Duanne said. Ida looked at her puny offspring. He didn't take after her side. "He can grow yet," she said unconvincingly.

"I'll work on the bypass, Mom," little Frankie said, "I'll learn how to drive heavy equipment."

"That's good, Frankie. Eat your ham so you get big and strong," Ida said.

"If you go to college you can do a lot of things," Duanne said.

"You name one kid in West Virginia that went to college and got a good job here," Ida said.

"George Boone went to college and he's the editor of the Gazette," Duanne said, shuffling the paper.

Ida took a section of the Hobbs Gazette from Duanne and said, "Look at this stuff: 'County to Spray for Mosquitos.'" She opened to the next page, "'Rob Taylor to run for Sheriff.' Now how's he going to be sheriff when he's even afraid to go hunting?" She turned the page to the Obituaries. Her mouth dropped open. "What? What is this? 'Ida Pilcher Dead at 40.' It's here under the obituaries, Duanne."

Duanne grabbed the paper back. "What's going on? Is that in the paper?" He read the whole obituary in a slow, confused tone, "Ida Pilcher, longtime resident of Hobbs, died unexpectedly of cardiac arrest at age 40 . . ." Duanne concluded the article ". . . She is survived by her husband, Duanne, and sons, Ernest and Frank."

"It's a mistake of some kind," he said, "I'll call the newspaper."

"What kind of joke is this?" Ida said. "Is this dead?" She stood up and held her arms out wide so everyone there could witness her fully functioning body.

"I'll call the Gazette." Duanne got up.

"No, let me call," Ida said. "I bet this is that Randy Beasley, Floyd's brother. He works over there. This is crazy." She and Duanne went into the living room and she dialed the Gazette, but the office was closed, so she looked up George Boone's number to call him at his house. Duanne went to answer a knock on the kitchen door. Ida could see old Mrs. Lowery, who volunteered at the Church of the Assembly, standing in the kitchen with a casserole dish, her eyes red and puffy. "I'm so sorry," she said to Duanne, "Your poor boys."

"It's a mistake, Mrs. Lowery," Duanne said, "It's a bad mistake." Mrs. Lowery who was hard of hearing continued to cry. She put the casserole on the table and threw her arms around Ernie and Frankie. Duanne turned to the living room toward Ida who was yelling on the phone, "What's wrong with you over there? Don't you check your facts? I can't believe you could be so ignorant." There was a pause for a few brief seconds but then she continued, "Don't give me that. I know it's that Randy Beasley's done this. I'm not going to take this. You're going to find that out."

Mrs. Lowery, still tearful in the kitchen, was trying to comfort the boys who continued to eat their dinner. Duanne was pacing from the kitchen to the living room and back again, rubbing the back of his neck. Little Frankie took some of the macaroni and cheese casserole that Mrs. Lowery had placed on the table.

Ida hung up the phone and went back to the kitchen, her face as red as the ham on the table. Mrs. Lowery put her hand to her mouth and gasped. Ida said, "Could you believe a newspaper could do such a thing?" She slammed it down on the table. "And you want your son to go into the newspaper business." Mrs. Lowery went over to Duanne and Ida and threw her arms around them and began singing, "Amazing Grace." Little Frankie joined in with her. Ernie laughed about the whole thing and Duanne and Ida stood there bewildered.

All evening Ida's phone rang with condolences that she accepted with the caveat that she was planning to remain around for thirty or forty more years. Mrs. Keegan from the Farmers Co-op brought over peach cobbler, and the Gazette sent over a fruit basket with an apology. Two funeral directors called, one of whom she could not convince that she was really in fine health. "All I ask is that you consider Murphy's Funeral Home when the time approaches," he said.

The next morning Ida called Lou. "Yes, I'm still alive, but I got me a migraine something awful over the whole thing."

"Take a couple of days off, Ida," Lou said. "You're very appreciated over here. We collected seventy-five dollars for flowers already. Should I send that to the American Heart Association like it said in the obituary?"

This threw Ida into a fury. As soon as she hung up she ran outside, got into her truck, and headed over to the Hobbs Gazette office on Main Street. She hardly even noticed the persistent vultures overhead with their dizzying swirls.

"I want a retraction on the first page with a recent photo so that people will stop sending me condolences, and I want to know whose idea of a joke this is. I would bet you anything it's that Randy Beasley," she said to George Boone.

"I don't know who put it in there, Ida," George said, "I proofread it but, honest to God, I really thought you passed. I was quite sad about the whole thing. I'll get to the bottom of it, and I promise I'll put your picture on the front page tonight with a complete retraction and an apology."

He phoned Mickey, the Gazette's photographer, and asked him to take a picture of Ida outside the Gazette building in front of the large digital date display. Ida followed him outside, and after a few snaps, she got in her Chevy truck and headed home to try to calm herself down. She lay on the living room couch with a cold washcloth on her forehead trying to recover from her continuing migraine.

Duanne came home about five with the paper in his hand and a look of gloom on his face. "What's wrong, Duanne? What's wrong?" He looked down at the paper. She pulled it from his hand to the horror of her picture on the front page with four vultures in view hovering over her head. The headline read, "Ida Pilcher Alive Despite Being Pursued by Vultures." The story was by Randy Beasley.

Ida hurried back to the Gazette before it closed and marched into George Boone's office. "I want that Randy Beasley fired for this story," she said shaking the front page at him. "He's doing this just because I wouldn't fix Floyd's TV."

"Well, this is a different twist now, Ida. If you've got a flock of vultures following you, that's real news. I never heard of such a thing. I just about have to report it or else I'm not doing my job. There's a lot of public interest in this story, I'm finding out. I got a lot of calls about it already. And people are concerned that more buzzards might start coming into Hobbs. You know, they regurgitate that stuff they eat and it's a real mess. The smell. Whew!"

"Now don't make it worse than it is. They haven't been regurgitating any and they've been hanging around my place for two weeks." She was sorry as soon as the words came out but continued, "I want that story retracted tomorrow, or I'm going to get Attorney Carney to sue your paper."

"I can't retract what's real news. Besides the Associated Press has already picked it up and put it on their wire. That's the first time that's happened to us here in Hobbs," he said with pride, "We could have other newspaper reporters out here even."

"Just expect to see Attorney Carney," Ida threatened and slammed the door to his office. She walked out of the Gazette and got into her truck with the vultures waiting for her. The lowest ones were just above the maple tree next to her truck, their red turkey heads staring down into her uplifted eyes.

"I'd like to wring your necks," she scowled at them.

When she got home she jumped out of her truck and stood there, legs akimbo, firmly planted on the ground, hands on her hips, looking up at the vultures swirling above her head. You can't win in this world, she thought. How could she control the entire sky. She'd like to kill the ugly beasts. She ran into the house and came out with Duanne's shotgun, raised it upward, and began shooting at the buzzards, but they just dispersed in a wide spiral. She chased after them yelling, "Get down here now, cowards." She kept shooting until she got one. It flopped down with a thud in the vegetable garden. Duanne came running out of the shop looking alarmed.

"I just shot one of those damn buzzards," she said,

glancing at him. "It's in the cabbage patch." She marched back toward the house.

"You can't shoot birds out of season. You know that," Duanne said, coming after her.

"That's not a bird. It's the devil from hell." She went into the house and slammed the door.

The next day an unfamiliar car pulled up to the farmhouse, and a stranger dressed in a tweed jacket and a turtleneck sweater got out. Ida observed him through one of the front windows. When he knocked, she opened the front door and stared at him through the locked screen door.

"Hello, I'm Professor Yates from West Virginia University. I've read about the vultures that are bothering you down here, and I thought I might be able to help out."

Ida sized him up and then opened the screen door. "C'mon in," she said, showing him into the parlor.

"Could you explain the whole situation?" the professor asked as he relaxed in her cushioned chair next to the fireplace. Ida perched on the sofa and went over every single detail.

"You know, sometimes birds are imprinted with someone who raises them or they see when they are born. Did you inadvertently coddle the birds, perhaps?"

Ida paused and then said piercingly, "They're buzzards, for God's sake. Why would I coddle a buzzard?"

"Look, I'm only trying to help," the professor said. He started rattling on about different cases where birds were imprinted with humans whom they took to be their parents. Ida stared at him thinking this was just a lot of stuff. He didn't know shit from shinola. She got up abruptly, "I gotta get to work. When you think of some way to get rid of these pests, come back." She ushered him out of her house.

Just as his car left, an SUV pulled up, and five men and women dressed almost entirely in shades of beige, with big brimmed hats and binoculars hanging around their necks, jumped out of the car like a swat team of park rangers and raised their binoculars to the sky.

Ida marched out to them. "What do you want around here?" she said.

"We're birders. We just came to see the vultures," one of them replied.

"You never seen a vulture before? They're all over the place. You don't have to come out here," she said. "This is a business here. If you don't want a hubcap, go someplace else to look for vultures."

"That could be it," one of the birders cried. "Some birds are attracted by shiny objects. They could be attracted by the hubcaps in your truck there." Ida looked over at the back of her old Chevy and the pile of gleaming hubcaps thrown in the back.

"Duanne has a lot of hubcaps in his truck. Why don't they follow him?"

"I don't know. Birds can be pretty peculiar. There's no accounting for some of their behavior. Once there were some starlings that crawled into the coin deposit box at a car wash and carried quarters in their beaks to the flat roof of the building. They found sixteen thousand quarters on the car wash roof after they set up a video cam and caught the birds right in the act. They may be attracted to the hubcaps because they gleam, or maybe they're attracted to a specific type of hubcap."

"So you don't know why they're following me?" Ida said.

"No. Not yet. But maybe something will come to us. We have a lot of bird experience here."

"Yeh, I can see that," she mumbled, opening the door of her truck. "Duanne will help you if you want to buy a hubcap."

The vultures followed her over to her truck, their menacing eyes stalking her every move, preparing to accompany her to town. One birder captured their departure with his video camera.

When she got to Lou's, the parking lot was filled with cars and reporters from the media.

"There she is," someone shouted. Snapping cameras trailed her as she ran into the shop past a mob of reporters blocking several of Lou's customers from carrying their TV's into the shop. After several days of this circus atmosphere, Ida agreed that for the good of Lou's business, she would take an extended vacation without pay.

But since she always believed in keeping busy, she decided to help Duanne organize his hubcap shop. "That's an H915 Mustang hubcap, Duanne. Don't put that there. It belongs on the 6E shelves. They're marked right here." Duanne frowned, but his business picked up since they were getting a lot of visitors who came just to see Ida's vultures, and Ida made a rule that any visitor that came within fifty feet of the place had to buy a hubcap.

Every birder, professor, reporter or sightseer who visited lined up to buy a hubcap. Sometimes the hubcap line stretched clear around the old oak tree on the other side of the house.

Duanne took advantage of the increase in sales by hitting the road to get more hubcaps from the junkyards and car dealers he used. Ida and Ernie worked in the store, and sometimes little Frankie set up a lemonade stand outside.

But in late October, birders and sightseers began to drop off, and Duanne became overstocked with hubcaps. The weather was getting gloomy as the seasons began to change, and Ida was miserable with nothing much to do and no one to talk to. Half the time Duanne and his buddies, Mo and Jake, went on the road trying to unload some of the excess hubcaps. And no one in Hobbs seemed much interested in visiting with the "Dead Vulture Lady" as people now referred to her. No one wanted to take a chance on having a vulture throw up on them with half-eaten carrion. That was the buzz around Hobbs, even though there was not one single incident of the kind.

One morning when Ida stopped for a doughnut at the Tasty Bakery, a few of the vultures descended ten feet above her head. Their beaks were open and the sheer size of them intimidated everyone near the Bakery. The entire parking lot cleared in five minutes with people screaming and dropping their doughnuts and coffee. After this, everyone avoided Ida and went the other way when they saw her coming as though she was possessed by demons or something. Even when she went to the Burger Boy at night for a fruit smoothie she could hardly get anyone to wait on her, much less join her for a little conversation.

Only the Indian woman, Shanti, treated her normally. "Fruit Smoothie?" she would ask with her perpetual smile, and Ida would say, "Yeh, the regular," and nod back with a slight grin. Sometimes Ida would go down to the Burger Boy late at night for a fruit smoothie just so she could have a pleasant exchange with someone.

One night near closing time Shanti came back to the corner booth where Ida was sitting and said, "You look very unhappy."

"I have my troubles," Ida said.

"In India we say accept your troubles and you will be at peace with the world," Shanti said, waving her right palm upward.

"Well, you see, I have these vultures that follow me everywhere I go. They're out there now," Ida said gesturing toward the parking lot. "What can I do about that?"

"I know about that," Shanti said cheerfully; "Just accept them. They are your vultures. They were sent to you only."

This sounded like a lot of stuff to Ida, but she said, "Maybe so." She slurped a little more of the smoothie and then said, "Well, I have to go now. Maybe I'll be back tomorrow."

Her life was miserable, day after day, week after week, with no companionship but her own family, and even they had become tight-lipped since their friends weren't coming around much. She never before believed in wasting time on being sad, but she was slipping into a deep melancholy.

One evening in early November Duanne and the boys were watching wrestling on TV. Ida looked at her watch and thought she might be able to make it to the Burger Boy before it closed.

Shanti came over to talk with her after she got her fruit smoothie. "I think it means you are very special."

"I don't want to be special, not like this," Ida said, but she began going to the Burger Boy nightly after that to talk to Shanti.

One day in late November, she went outside and looked up at the vultures, lifted her hands up in the air like some kind of preacher, and shouted, "O.K. I accept you vultures. I accept you as my own."

Duanne came rushing out of the shop, "What was that?"

"Nothing, Duanne." She continued to look up at the swirling vultures. "I was just accepting my vultures like the Indians do." Duanne shook his head sideways with a grim look and went back in the shop.

The first snow of the season fell that night. When Ida got up in the morning, Duanne was outside already with his snow blower clearing the parking lot in front of his shop. Ida came out bundled up to see how bad it was, and out of habit she and Duanne looked up for her vultures. After a good ten minutes there were still no vultures, not one. Duanne smiled, "They're gone, Ida."

"I don't see them anywhere," she said, circling around the lot in the snow. She went over to her truck to see if they would show up there. She couldn't find any.

"Thank God, they're gone, finally," Duanne said. He jumped up and down in the snow cheering wildly for a few minutes.

But Ida had just accepted her vultures as Shanti told her, and now they were gone. Maybe they were gone because she accepted them, she thought. Or would they come back? And then what? Would she go through this again?

She leaned against her Chevy pickup, gazed at the bleak gray sky and the mountains and fields all around her covered in snow, and felt relieved despite her doubts. As soon as the snow was plowed, she would go to the Burger Boy and see what Shanti thought about it all.

~

Half of the human race laughs at the expense
of the other half. – Destouches

Writing on the Wall

Jeff Vande Zande

Walt was always reading something. Standing with the current of the Au Sable's South Branch moving around his thighs, he read the river. The stretch ahead was wide and flat and without riffles. The small, lazy rises near the edges were probably just creek chubs. Fifty yards later, the river narrowed at a bend, and the surface began to flash white with its roughening before it turned out of sight. Just beyond the bend there was a tree down in the water on the left bank and beyond the scum line of the tree a nice hole. He'd finessed a thirteen-inch brookie out of the hole the year before. Thinking of the fish, he pulled his heavy feet from the mucky bottom where they'd settled.

He carried a cloth glove to handle each fish, having read that it was less likely to strip away its protective mucous. Dipping the glove through the surface, he'd hold the fish while gently removing the hook with his forceps. He pinched his barbs flat, so his hooks slipped out easily. Balancing his catch lightly between his thumb and fingers, he'd set it just below the surface in a calm part of the river. He'd stand stooped until the fish would find its bearings and swim out of his palm. It's what he'd done with the brookie the year before. It's what he'd do with any fish. He didn't come to the river to keep fish. He came to forget, even if only for just a few hours.

For others, the river had become a battleground. He couldn't help but read about it. It was in all the fly fishing magazines. Some company in Traverse City owned the mineral rights to the land around the river. They wanted to drill for natural gas and other resources. Fly fishing organizations were fighting it. They called the area sacred and wrote lengthy arguments and raised money. They won the first court battle, but as recently as six months ago it looked likely that the ruling might be overturned in the company's favor. Walt started ignoring articles that dealt with the controversy. After all, the company owned the mineral rights. It struck him as a no-brainer. Fighting. Politics. It wasn't what he wanted on his mind when he came to the river.

He rubbed his eyes, took a long breath, and then started downstream. The sun was close to moving below the trees in the west. The day was cooling. Walt cast to some likely spots and felt the way the rituals of fishing filled his consciousness. Rises. Cover. Hatches. Riffles. They were simple thoughts, but they held off everything else.

He'd only moved a short distance when he noticed another fisherman at the bend below. A footpath ran along the river, and fishermen could pop in anywhere. Walt forced his disappointment down. The new man had as much right to the water as he did. The stranger might be bringing his own heaviness to the river, his own need to forget.

After a moment, the new man wristed his first cast. Walt's disappointment welled up again and soon became anger. He hooked his fly into the hook keeper, wound up his slack, and marched toward the man. Walt had read about such men in different fly fishing magazines. This was the first time he'd seen one.

The new man turned, and his face blanched. Looking Walt over for a few seconds, he tried to smile. He touched his palm to his chest. "Man, scared me," he said. "Thought you were maybe DNR."

Walt looked at the open-faced spinning reel on the other man's pole. He then turned his stare up into the man's face. "What kind of *fly* do you have on?"

The other man turned his hand and looked at his reel. A Mepps spinner dangled and dripped at the end of his line. He looked at Walt and started to grin sheepishly.

"This is flies only," Walt said, pointing at the river.

The other man was bigger than Walt, thicker. Some of the color came back into his face. He stiffened his jaw. "So," he returned.

Walt stepped over to the bank and laid his rod in the grass. He came back to the man. Both of his hands were free, and he knotted them into fists and kept them steady at his sides. "So," he repeated back to the man. "So, I'll take you apart right here."

The river moved around the legs of the men. A wind pushed through the higher branches of the trees. It stirred nothing at their level.

"You're serious," the man said. He blinked. "You're serious?"

Walt didn't release his fists. "This is flies only."

The other man couldn't keep any kind of eye contact. Paling again, he released his line and groped for his spinner. His voice was an octave higher when he spoke. "I mean, I just wanted to take a fish home. No big deal." He set one of the treble hooks into the biggest eye on his pole and gave the reel a few turns. The tip of the pole bent. "It's just that I don't live far from here. It's easy to get to after work."

"It's not right. It's illegal."

"All right," the other man said, holding up an apologetic palm. He started toward the bank, beyond which was the footpath. "Well, good luck fishing," he said awkwardly.

Walt retrieved his rod and watched the other man flash here and there through the woods until he was gone. His heart writhed in his ribs like a dying fish in a creel.

He was a different man from what he'd ever been. Just the week before, in the middle of a sales call, he looked across the desk at the young man who was studying a contract that Walt had given him. "Can't really afford a television ad," the young man said, "but this seems reasonable." He owned a new bookstore, and he was wearing a t-shirt with the name of the store on it. It had been open for a month and a half, and he'd already had t-shirts printed up. Walt had talked him into a month's worth of radio spots. Probably could have talked him into a year's worth. "You know," Walt confessed, "our listeners aren't really book people. We've surveyed them, and they don't read." The young man set his pen down. His smile faded. "Then I shouldn't do this?" Walt shook his head. "You shouldn't."

He had a meeting coming up with the radio station's manager and guessed that they would be talking about his miserable sales numbers. Walt's son had been dead for over a year and a half. His dying was losing some of its strength as an excuse.

Walt had read somewhere that few marriages survive the death of a child. Knowing that what he and his wife had gone through was typical didn't bring him any comfort. He was alone. She was gone, living in a spare room in the basement of her parents' place. Sometimes he'd talk to her on the phone. There was so little of her left that he'd sob after hanging up.

He'd lost them both. He stood in the river going numb, the water pushing against his legs as though they were two rotted trunks ready to fall.

Downstream, just past a long stretch of riffled water, a trout rose in the crook of one of the river's elbows. It was a slow, confident rise in the kind of bend where a big trout might linger, waiting for the fast water to wash in feed. The surface where the fish had risen turned in a slow eddy. Perfect.

The fish came up three more times before Walt was able to get within casting distance. They were so consistent he could almost time the rises. He studied the surface. There didn't seem to be a hatch going on. He stayed with his blue-winged olive – a trustworthy fly for almost any Michigan river. Casting upstream of the hole, he let the fly drift naturally across the surface of it.

Nothing.

Not wanting to spook the fish, he waited until the fly and his line had drifted well past the hole before he tried another cast. The first cast might have been too far from the bank. Hadn't the fish been feeding closer to the partially submerged rock? Walt wasn't sure. He cast again. And again. "What the hell do you want me to do," he said ten minutes later, "put steak sauce on the damn thing?"

He tried two other flies before abandoning the hole. The fish had been seemingly going after anything. And then a blue-winged olive, a mosquito, and a royal coachman drifted right over it within a twenty-minute span. Why wouldn't it come up? How did it know? Leaving the hole, Walt felt a tickling of anger. He suppressed it. The frustrated questions he was posing about the nature of fish were gentle compared to others he could ask about the nature of life.

He'd fished for two hours already and hadn't seen a cabin. The Mason Tract – nothing but wilderness and river. He had read about George Mason and the donation of property the auto executive had made to the state of Michigan. Fourteen miles of river and the adjacent land given over for public use.

Walt looked around. The river. The trees. The sky above. All of it was darkening toward night. He remembered a book, an old book – maybe even the Bible – which he'd been made to read as a teenager. There was something in it about going to the woods to live deliberately. Something too about quiet desperation. His own desperation felt anything but quiet. It pleased him when his mind put together the sentence, "I went to the woods to live forgetfully." He'd always liked putting words together and had once used the skill to write radio spots.

Living forgetfully. It was a bliss, a reprieve. The water swirling around his thighs might well have been the Lethe River, given the merciful amnesia it cast over him.

In the current at times like this he sometimes felt something around him – something bigger than the trees and the river. Something bigger than him, something he had never been able to name with any confidence, and yet a presence. It was the something that for the longest time he'd blamed for his son's death. It was the something, too, that he thanked on nights like this for making water move.

Walt tied on a new leader and a new fly – a pattern of his own making. He used a size 8 hook, black thread and dubbing for a body, dun hackle, and finally deer tail to make a large, white parachute wing. He squeezed fly dressing between his thumb and forefinger and pinched it over the hackle. The fly glinted with the floatant. For a short time it would be easier for Walt to see without the glare of the setting sun on the surface. Then it would get dark. It was coming into the time when he often caught a better-sized fish. He worked the stretches along the bank.

Something glowed orange on his left. A man was sitting on a log smoking a cigar. He was gray-haired and had a fly rod and wicker creel. Walt smiled when the older man nodded. The other man's waders were shiny with water. Smoke drifted up.

"Just getting in?" Walt asked above the talking of the river.

The other man brought the cigar to his mouth, took a puff, and shook his head. "Been here since noon. Just getting done."

"Can't find your car?" Walt asked, smiling.

The other man grinned, and the tip of his cigar flared in front of his face. He exhaled languorously. "Just not ready to go home yet."

Walt nodded, knowing the feeling. He waved a mosquito from his face. "Fishing good?"

"Fishing's always good."

"Yeah," Walt said.

He fished on and soon had trouble seeing. Fishing at night took from him one of his favorite aspects of fly fishing. He liked to watch his fly. He liked to see it when a fish rose and pulled it under. It was a part of everything that made fishing good for him. With the darkness fading in around him, he became aware of the dark thoughts crowding into his mind. He didn't want them. The Fisherman's Chapel was just around the next bend. He would get out of the water there.

There was no moon. Walt caught his breath after climbing

the flight of stairs. The inside of the chapel was like a cave. What he'd read only a few days before was haunting him again. The article had been in one of the magazines in the radio station's lobby. He had tried to abandon the words when he could see where they were going. It was no use. He couldn't stop reading. It related that by nine years old children understand death and can anticipate their own. They can live their last hour in the terrifying fear of knowing that it will be their last hour.

Standing in the blackness of the chapel, he imagined his son, his little Tommy, treading water in the bottom of the well. It was Walt's idea to move the family to the country. He had wanted the old property and had even found the ancient well charming . . . as charming as the skeletal remains of the old Nash rusting to nothingness in the woods behind the property. He and his wife had warned Tommy about the well so many times. How could it have been that after two days of searching that's where they'd found his waterlogged body? How many times had the boy called up the shaft of the well, and heard as a reply only the echo of his voice coming off the wooden curbing? Treading in the cold, Tommy knew he was going to die.

Walt dropped to his knees and cried into his palms. He lived in the sobbing like he had lived in the fishing. It consumed everything.

In time, he held out a hand and steadied his shaking body against a wooden beam. His fingers found something. Someone had carved something deep into the wood. He traced his fingers along what turned out to be letters and spelled out the word *faith*. Searching above the word, he touched along more jack-knifed Braille and found the other word. *Have.*

Have faith. How many times had he read it in sympathy cards or heard it as consolation from family and friends? Have faith. In what? In the cruelty of life? In its ephemeral nature? Have faith that in the end our lot is suffering and that everything we build up and come to cherish will be slowly or quickly taken from us? He fought these black thoughts. Tonight, having found the words, he wanted them to mean something. He recalled the peace he'd felt on the river, the cleansing. Staying on his knees for a long time, he turned the phrase over in his mind, waiting for something.

Walt stepped out of the chapel. Releasing his tears had done him good, and he felt loosened. Above the blackness, in the spaces between the trees, he found the sky speckled like a trout. And, listening for it, he heard the river whispering in the valley below. They were things he could trust and the sight and sound of them buoyed him. He still had the wade upstream through the darkness toward the car. The river would be at his legs. It seemed a small burden considering what the water had given him that night.

While he stood in the darkness, another sound came to him when he stopped straining to hear the river. It was a noise that he'd been dimly aware of earlier. It wasn't like any sound he'd heard before in the woods. It droned and hummed with a measured, consistent rhythm that wasn't natural. It came from beyond the bluff above, and he guessed immediately what the source would be.

His rod caught against branches as he clawed his way up the hillside. His waders slowed him. When he crested the top, the mechanical noise was still there. He stood listening to it and feeling the sweat cooling around his ribs. In the distance, through the woods, a pale light glowed ghostly. He headed for it.

Soon, he could see it through the trees. The company had won. They won. He stumbled out into a sudden opening in the woods. An acre of timber had been clear cut around the well site, and a dirt road disappeared toward the south into the darkness. They'd squared a twelve-foot high chain-link fence around the pump, and a street light glowed down on it from a freshly planted light pole. The ground looked wounded.

The pump made a racket resonant of the sounds that would wake him when he and his wife were young and their apartment was near a rail yard. It looked futuristic and prehistoric at the same time – the steel, birdlike head dropping down and coming up. Down and up. Down and up. Endless in its hunger. Something about its dinosaur-like build brought up ideas of extinction.

He remembered some of the arguments he'd read. One fisherman pointed out that a little used two-track would be widened into a byway for heavy trucking. Walt looked at the road again, obviously ripped in recently by earthmoving equipment. The roots of upended trees groped into the blackness along the sides of the road. He remembered something too about the risk of brine or chemical spills into Singer, Sanger, and Sauger Creeks – all three of which fed right into the South Branch. Fishermen and environmentalists argued that if the first well were successful, more would follow.

Other memories of what he'd read came into his mind. Most of Michigan's waters had once held trout – even the Detroit's Rouge River before the city began treating the stream like a urethra for all its waste and refuse. Industry had come in and made many rivers too slow, warm, and poisonous to sustain such precious life. It wasn't just the southern rivers that suffered. Fertilizer ran off from farms and golf courses into feeder streams up north. It happened everywhere in the state.

Walt thought also of the long dorsal fin on an arctic grayling, a fish he had only seen in books. It had once thrived in the Au Sable system until reckless logging destroyed its spawning habitat.

He squeezed his hands into fists. This place was supposed to be sacred, a gift. Hunching over, he searched the ground and came up with a rock the size of a softball, cold and earthy. Hurled over the fence, it clanged thunderously against the steel.

The pump kept on. Down and up. It was much stronger than some glass-jawed Goliath. Listening for the river or for the wind, Walt heard nothing except for the pump. He studied it for a long time.

He always kept a piece of paper folded in his vest pocket to write things down to remember for his next trip. During the last trip, he'd written down *tippet*, and he could feel the thin spool in his upper vest pocket. The list helped him remember. He looked at the cyclone fencing around the well site. He took out the piece of paper, unfolded it, and fished out the stub of pencil. He wrote down *bolt cutters*. Under it, he wrote *monkey wrench*.

~

Alas for human life! In prosperity 'tis but a sketch,
and when misfortune comes, the wet sponge with a touch
blots out the drawing. – Aeschylus

Suspended Lines

James K. Zimmerman

We were on the lake by about eight in the morning in a motorized canoe rented from the outfitter. We had lures – plugs for walleyes, poppers for bass – and corpulent night-crawlers for the crappies. I hadn't slept well because sharing a room with my father I'd been exposed to his stentorian, jagged snoring all night, but breakfast had been good and big and Southern (even including a very adult cup of coffee). Digestion wasn't as good because of my father's typical disgruntled attitude toward the waiter, who had made the egregious error of bringing to the table a fork that was apparently not immaculately clean.

The silence between us going out to the fishing spot was acceptable because the canoe's motor sputtered and choked, making conversation difficult if not impossible. On some level, I knew this trip was an attempt on my father's part to connect to his tentative, sullen, distant son, and I wasn't so sure I wanted to oblige. In fact, at fourteen, I *was* sure that I was unwilling to risk saying or doing the wrong thing, incurring his sudden explosive outbursts of anger. Long ago, I had lost respect for him; by now, combined with adolescent hubris, it sometimes bordered on disdain or disgust.

We fished for hours in the filtered sunlight, eating our sandwiches in discomfort amid the cramped confines of the boat and our awkwardness with each other, drinking our Dr. Pepper out of the bottle. Communication was limited to fish talk – Was that a rise over there? You see that stick-up? I bet there's a school of tasty crappies. Let's try for a bass in the weeds – and so on. Glances at each other were sidelong, fleeting. Attention was focused on tying on a new lure, untangling a line, or re-worming the hook. With shoulders hunched and tense, I found myself anticipating my father's disapproval: "Goddamnit, can't you tie on a lure without dropping it?"

We found a fallen tree trunk, which my father knew from long experience was a likely place for crappies and other school-fish. We threw in our lines and, within fifteen minutes, caught eight good-size crappies. The excitement grew – this was a personal record for us – and along with it a subtle thawing and occasional quick, shy smile. As we caught them, we hooked them on the stringer: "Crappies are good eating, good eating – but they're really dumb. They just about crawl up the line into the boat. Let's go for a bass."

So we aimed toward the shore, the lily pads where bass lurk, motor off so as not to disturb the waters, I in the bow and my father in the stern. Again, I could feel the tension in my shoulders, my back, less from the work at hand than from a lifelong wariness and foreboding. I thought I saw a log ahead; I shifted my paddle from the left to the right side of the canoe to avoid it. The invective came: "Jesus Christ, keep your paddle on one side so I can steer!" – "But I was only trying to . . ." – "Just *do* it!"

We neared the shore in pained silence. (It was only many years later that I realized how ashamed my father was of his own inability to control his temper.) The day felt ruined somehow, even with the string of crappies flapping and splashing alongside the gunnel. We slid our paddles into the belly of the canoe and picked up our rods. My father sent a singing cast deep in among the lily-pads; I flipped the bale over too early, so mine swung clumsily through the air and smacked back into the side of the boat. "Je . . ." For once, he stopped himself.

After a few more desultory attempts, I got one decent cast out. As I was reeling in, the popper creating a series of satisfying *bloops* and ripples on the lake's surface, my father said: "Let me just pull in this last big one." This was a ritual on all fishing trips, expressing both the hope of catching a trophy bass and the hapless way in which things usually turned out. I was expected to laugh at the joke: I half-grinned, anxious and sarcastic. As I watched, my father snapped the metal lure out across the lake, deftly, smoothly. It landed in the water, thirty yards from the canoe, with a faint *sploop*.

The sound echoed limpidly in the pines across the lake. The pungent, rotting smell of the lake's edge seemed suddenly a little sweeter, the air more still, hushed. "Will you look at that!" my father said, more of an awed whisper than a shout. Yes, I saw it: the line stayed suspended in the air, billowing like the forward edge of a schooner's sail luffing in becalmed waters. In the late afternoon light, it etched the rippling arc the weighted lure had followed, without falling into the taut, straight hypotenuse gravity would demand. We looked at the line, gently waving in the delicate breeze, then at each other. "That is really amazing," I thought. We smiled. A rush of energy rose up my spine, blooming on cheeks that had not yet felt the tug of a razor. "That is really amazing," I said.

After an appreciable time – seconds or minutes, I don't know – my father began slowly, regretfully, cranking the reel. The bale clicked over, the reel sang, and immediately, the line again cooperated with Newtonian laws of physics. The lure arrived at the boat with no fish struggling to spit it out, but that didn't seem to matter so much anymore. We packed in the rods and reels in silence, reverently picked up our paddles (the motor would have been a sacrilege), slid them into the water simultaneously, and began meandering back to the outfitter's kitchen and a feast of fresh crappies.

A cluster of spring peepers began their sweet, liquid chant, greeting the first stars in the evening sky. Others joined in, a few at a time, until the shorelines around us were a swirling galaxy of song. Even a lone bullfrog offered his bellowing croak as a counterpoint to the celestial soprano of his tiny cousins.

And the air had changed: there was warmth in it that should have faded with the sunlight; there was a closeness that was not uncomfortable. My shoulders seemed not quite as knotted as before, my neck less tight. I kept my paddle on one side of the canoe and felt somehow stronger, more graceful and mature. My father said nothing, but I could feel his paddle at my back moving in rhythm with mine. The canoe's path through the water was sinuous, gliding in harmony with the evening ripple on the lake, drawing us into the golden glow of the cabin lights on the shore.

The Son's Complaint

Anne Whitehouse

A boy toboggans down a white hill. The red slash of his coat rushes past trees. In the deaf world, he encounters nothing living but himself and the solid trees.

So began the recurring dream of the child of the family, who, when awake, sat in the insulated basement reading his books and papers. The books were scientific treatises that he pored over, for he'd been taught they were keys to enlightenment. He sought to uncover the epistemological bases of abstract systems. He pondered tragic error. His mother, who aspired to be the guardian of genealogical record, had assembled the papers, which were the surviving documents of the family's history. In old photographs, he studied the dour images of his ancestors. Their faded correspondence, detailed with inventions and projects, became his basement bulwark. The ceiling vibrated under the heavy steps of his brothers. Heat rose in the thick pipes.

Can the lost son be restored?

The father's hobby was collecting measurements and statistics on animals. They were published in an elaborate book with painted illustrations of their living or extinct subjects. Turning the gilt-edged pages of the book, it was impossible not to notice the contortions each beast assumed to fit the page. In the unfilled spaces floated islands of numbers.

Attached to themselves, the numbers squirmed and

wriggled. Once they had been fixed and black; now they paled, grey as lint. They were growing invisible.

The father pretended he could still see them, but his children believed he was lying.

As the numbers evaded him, the father persisted in his claims. Only the bright illustrations still riveted his eyes. Before their gay colors, he grew morose. He grasped a leaf of the book, his arm jerked, and a jagged tear grew down the page. His hand curved like a claw over the ruined picture.

One by one, he tore the pages from his book. They settled like chips on the scratchy plain of the rug.

All this time the child of the family had remained below. He imagined the cries of the lost animals. He despaired of changing anything. He believed he was the unexcavated heart whose ticking kept the house whole. Above him, his father stamped and raged.

In his dream, the bushes stick out of the snow like wires. He skims over the world, past the dense black trunks of trees. If only he could evade it all, nothing to touch him or make him stop. Eventually the landscape blots out, and he travels with only the swoosh of his motion and the snow-spray falling back into his face. Behind him, his blue shadow, longer and soundless.

He has always been smaller than everyone. At first he was ashamed of his weakness, of his skinny arms that curled like ribbons. He never thought they could hold onto anything. He tried to cultivate his mind as compensation.

He believed his position was inevitable. The bare light bulb trembled above his head. He was wrapped in blankets, lying on a couch, and the rough texture of the material irritated his frail neck. Would the words in his books prove as elusive as his father's numbers? He tried to fix them with a look, with a will that surprised him as much as his father's rage, but it seemed to him they devoured him, like tapeworms feeding on his brains.

He read the accounts of his ancestors, who once had advanced their monologue against the wilderness. He imagined the purple smoke from their riverbank campfires in rich autumn and their hands stained from the forest berries.

One man carved bowls from solid oak, some big enough to hold a baby, which he peddled downstream in his canoe. Once he hit a floating log, the boat overturned, and the bowls floated away from him, their hollowed crescents facing skyward like lily pads. Some he retrieved; some filled with muck and were caught frozen till spring; others perhaps washed ashore at a stranger's landing.

After these vagabonds, the son stayed put. Wandering was useless when wide paved roads divided the continent. No matter where he might move, he would find the land already owned and parceled, so he contemplated the vanished past and read the diaries and letters of his dead, distant relatives.

~

On certain fixed occasions, the family gathered for a ritual meal. Small talk and clinking glasses filled the living room, where, under a flower-printed sofa and chairs, the green lawn of a rug covered the floor: domesticated outdoors. The grown children balanced on the edges of their chairs, sipping fiery drinks that brought on thirst. When the gong rang, they removed themselves to the dining table. Steam rose from the uncovered dishes and slowly worked into their eyes. The father had lounged while his wife shopped and cooked; now the rites were all his.

First was the ceremony of dismembering the meat. The side of an animal dominated the table. Brown juice ran down the crinkled fat and over the ribs that once had protected the animal's heart. The father wielded the steel; the brown-crusted slices piled up on the plate. He apportioned the servings of the expensive meal his earnings had purchased.

Except for the last son, the children's growth surpassed their parents'. They required more sustenance than formerly; still they did not enjoy the thick meat. The chewed fibers caught between their teeth, but they ate more. Their lips glistened, dark wine shone blood-red on teeth and palate and stained the corners of their mouths.

Outside the snow seemed to drop from nowhere. It settled and whirled up and settled again in the same place. As the children ate, they recalled the names of extinct animals; they described the poisoning of marsh and forest, lake and river, as if they were discussing a patient whose prognosis they'd already judged fatal. It could be argued that even the food they were eating had been poisoned. Under their clothes, their skin was blotched with sweat; the house's painted walls were warm to the touch. They criticized the interior heat that made an artificial summer in the winter's midst. Rinds of fat curled on their plates. Licking their forks, shaking the last drops of wine down their throats, they decried the flagrance of their father's waste.

A hum vibrated in the mother's throat. She wanted to drown her children's accusations. Her nervous smile never reached her eyes. In a high, piercing voice, she tried to coax her family into agreement. The ruby jelly quivered in the glass.

But the father would not be placated. He reiterated his rights. Once his large children had cowered before his will;

now they felt a sadness beyond rancor. Although he fed them, he still denied them.

Like his brothers, the child of the family had eaten. He laid his silver across his plate. He looked outside: the mercury had climbed, and a hesitant rain fell on the snow. The others left the table, their big feet printing the rug's pile. Worn out by the meal, the father napped on the couch. Alone, the son stood in the empty dining room.

No one living wanted to know him for what he was. He thought he forgot himself, just as he'd thought, after his long basement sojourn, he no longer recalled the sound of rain falling on the roof. Yet, he found he not only remembered but anticipated the animal-like hiss of the dropping rain. He felt an earlier self listening, too, more timid and capable of wonder, watching the blank-windowed houses, the round bushes, the poles of trees, and unrelieved flatness of the yard and the street. A lattice of branches veined the sky. The windless rain left pockmarks in the melting snow.

It was then that they came back, the dead relatives, while his father slept in the living room, the dishes clattered from his mother's fingers into the dishwasher, and his brothers took their boisterous ire into another part of the house. A man in a stovepipe hat stood under a lantern in the yard; the light fell in slanting rays on the snow, illumining the gentle, silent rain. The man was smoking an elaborate, curved pipe. The son recognized him from photographs: inventor of several useful machines, entrepreneur and family autocrat, from whom survived a long, vitriolic letter, wordy with self-righteousness, reproaching a wastrel younger brother. Through the window glass, the son heard him tap his pipe against the steel lamppost. A faint pink haze hung in the air, perhaps a reflection off the snow. The man was silent, as befits the dead. After emptying the bowl, he slipped his pipe into his breast pocket and, looking left and right, crossed the empty street and disappeared from the son's view. A woman came next, running, almost tripping on her long skirts. She carried an umbrella that rose and fell with her exertions. She, too, paused under the lantern. Oval raindrops slowly slid down the hollows between the umbrella's ribs. She was looking at the house. How close she seemed! The son saw how the loose wisps of her hair had collected droplets of moisture. She turned toward the window where he watched, his nose flattened against the glass, his features dark, the light behind him. She nodded. He couldn't mistake her invitation. He didn't recognize her face from any family album, lovely in a soft way his people never had.

Her cheek glistened; he was utterly still. Her face was near, but her smile was as distant as pale spring. She seemed about to step toward him, when, from the periphery of his vision, the man returned, walking with a swift frontier gait. He took her arm, whether lightly or cruelly, the son couldn't tell. Just once, she glanced back at the pure circle of light on the shrinking snow.

He didn't mean, at first, to go outside; he was wearing tennis shoes. Like a sponge, the snow had filled with rainwater. He sloshed through the front yard, under the wet maples. How quiet it was, even his footsteps. Thick clouds hid the moon; the rain had turned to mist.

The night had found him; he no longer wanted to pursue them. This was the whiteness precipitated in the year's black core. The cold soothed his eyes, weary from reading. When his brothers had said that the world was poisoned, he had believed them and participated in their indictment of the parents. Now he found the world held in a spell-like paralysis, nearly stilled to the immobility of a photograph, inhospitable, still beautiful.

In the mist, not a star was visible. No longer certain of his brief visitors, he went inside. No one saw him. He crept down to the basement and fell asleep.

~

He dreamed again of the toboggan flying down the white hill. He lunged in a pure ecstasy of motion, and this time the slope flattened; he went farther, he reached the end, and the world returned to him in its sharp detail. Abruptly, the toboggan stopped, mired in level snow. He got up, brushed the loose snow off himself, shook his muffler and emptied his cap. The toboggan's rope in his mittened hand, he trudged past a frozen pond, blurred as bottle glass, and into a wood whose twisting contours were as familiar as the lines across his palm. His hands and feet were freezing. The woods climbed a hillside; a woodpecker bored into a dead tree so nearly above him that his wool cap caught a falling chip.

He emerged into a field rutted by absent wagons. The sky was an intense blue, absolutely empty. No plants had broken through this snow. He had grown smaller, a small boy. From here it was not too far to the street of ranch-style houses: past a ravine, a creek still flowing under a skin of ice, and then the fenced, familiar backyards – corner gardens lumping the snow, the frosted poles of swing sets and the slick, dangling seats.

In the house in front of him, a door opened. A woman's back pushed out a second screen door. She was only wearing an apron over her housedress, and she staggered with a full tub, which she heaved and emptied out onto the yard, a little waterfall of grayish, sudsy water. They both watched the water sink in the snow, leaving bubbles like spume on a beach of white sand. As she turned back to the house, he heard his own voice call her, "Mother."

She stopped and waited, seeing him. He unlatched the gate and pulled in his toboggan behind him. She knelt so they were eye to eye in the doorway, touching. She removed his cap, unwound his muffler to a long red strip, and unfastened his coat, button by button. While she unlaced his boots, he gripped her shoulder for support. One at a time, she slipped them off his cold feet. She took off his shirt, his pants. He trembled in the open doorway, and she hugged him around his waist. The cotton and woolen garments piled softly on the floor behind her. He stood naked in her grasp that wouldn't let him into the warm house, the cold breath of the snowy backyard tingling his bare back.

He awoke twisted in blankets, fretful and frightened. He shivered, remembering the dreamt moment of his exposure.

He heard his father, his mother, his brothers calling him.

His mother saw the extending family as figures blurring into each other, inexact yet authentic reproductions. She loved finding similarities over breached time. Her children were inextricably connected, not only to her and to their father, but to the long procession of the family's past.

His brothers were waiting for him around the cold fireplace, their arms folded across their chests in disapproval. A shifting alliance was now ranged against him. He looked up to see if his brothers' faces were joined by those of his parents, but his mother and father were missing. Slowly he grew aware of them, standing behind his turned back, watching dimly from the hallway outside the room. He didn't know who had initiated this summons.

"You were never with us," his brothers complained in unison. They enumerated his sin of neglect, his preference for solitude, his lack of familial ties, and, most grievous of all, his flouting of duty. He stood before them on the green rug, head lowered and hands clasped behind him like a prisoner. What divided him joined them. Outside the window – darkness, the lantern and its misted penumbra, the dissolving snow. His eye went from that scene to this scene surreptitiously, for his brothers were still talking and expected his attention.

In his mind he saw again the torn pages of his father's book, tropically bright. He heard the beating of wings, a wind through leaves, water rippling. He saw the sun on the rocks and felt the radiant heat.

His power existed because it was unknown. In the basement, under their echoing steps, he had his secrets, and in the winter night, he had them, too. When his brothers ceased talking, he sat down and stared into the empty fireplace. He could picture the licking flames in his head; he could conjure anything.

~

Each contact with a human being is so rare, so precious,
one should preserve it. — Anaïs Nin

Conversation With a Tree

Janyce Stefan-Cole

I want to tell you something that might make me sound crazy. I'm guessing you will read on because you won't be able to help yourself. My former husband John said I was too intense. He didn't use the term inward gaze, but that's what he meant. And he didn't say crazy.

Here goes: I'm seated in the sunroom next to a pile of research books on a developmental disorder, stretched out on the chaise, and a few minutes ago I looked up from my reading to hear the tree outside the window speak. Are you still there? I'll change the subject for a moment to let the idea sink in. Sometimes looking away is the best way to see.

The sunroom is also known as the tripping room. My friend Andy gave it that name because it's a pentagon with four gigantic windows that look out onto fields and mountains beyond. The sunset views are spectacular, and it's a perfect room for smoking pot or eating hallucinogens. Andy is a musician, and that's all I'll say on mood altering stimulants because you'll be tempted to think I was high on something just now when the tree spoke. But no, I'm sober as death, a blanket wrapped over my lap since the summer day has turned chilly. Mists shroud the mountains, making them resemble a Chinese landscape painting, partially veiled in white.

When the tree spoke, a cold dart of fear shot through my bowels. It's a fir; tall, offering generous shade on hot afternoons. Seen from outside, the tree is perfectly shaped and could be an easy mark for sacrifice to the Rockefeller Center Christmas display. I was stalling just now. Trees cannot speak, right? But this one did say the following sentence:

"I am here in the rain."

You know it's raining? I mentally asked back. The tree said so, but I had trouble accepting that level of awareness. I know of certain hallucinogens that might make a person *think* they hear trees speak, that encourage the perception of interconnectedness among all things, like a luminous web at the sub-atomic level stringing all that is together into a long cosmic necklace. Peyote is a good example used by certain Central American Indian tribes for religious purposes.

I have not heard a tree speak in the city. What about the cosmic necklace there? Are cities so dense and out of touch with whatever the saliva or plasma is that holds us all together that a kind of deafness sets in? This is my first summer alone up here and the questions just come and go. Maybe the country air, while expanding my lungs and appetite, is loosening the gum of my sanity. Did the tree speak or not?

My first instinct was denial. I do it all the time. One of my choicer ways to get through what could potentially be an insulting situation is to pretend nothing happened. For example, I said nothing recently when a colleague suggested I was conventional in my research. And when he said on another occasion I was a romantic, I did not take up that challenge either. The way I see it, had I chosen to take exception we might have spiraled into hairsplitting realms of meanings and effects. Endless clarifications could have followed and possibly deeper misunderstanding and even regrettable words exchanged. So I let it ride. Now, theoretically, people with the mental disorder I am researching have no concept of an insult – either given or received. Think of that for a moment: no greed, envy, covetousness, hatred, no deceit or any of the other lovely characteristics that work so hard to make us all so miserable.

I'll return to the point. Here is where we are: me sitting very still in the pentagon room, safe from the now heavily falling rain, but apparently not from trees sneaking up with a new reality. I know I'm asking for a leap of faith. I don't like this any more than you do. I considered leaving, driving back to my concrete city apartment. The country house is made of wood that has been cut from trees like the one outside, milled and hammered and made to stand so people can walk and sleep and talk inside them. I worry sometimes, way back in a far corner of my mind about the comforts and pleasures we take at the expense of others, *plants* and people. I don't have answers to questions that have haunted great minds through the centuries. I have preferences, free range eggs and pure cashmere, *Cotes du Rhône* over *Merlot*, for example. But answers would require greater certainty about many things, none of which has anything to do with trees talking.

I am in the country alone and you are probably thinking, too alone. I mentioned my ex. Sadly, John grew into someone smug and uncharitable who made me feel afraid to express myself. I didn't see this in him at first and can't be certain if he changed or if I had been blinded by his deep gray eyes, but even my mother agreed he had to go. I got the country house in the settlement; he got the brownstone with the wine cellar. By now it should be clear that I am not an inexperienced woman suddenly hearing things. I was hesitating to be too assertive, but the tree *did* speak.

Looking at the muted tree line, the misty mountains beyond, hearing the birds twitter, less in the damp, but going about their daily business nevertheless, I see a very real landscape, not a web of threads through the belly button of all that lies before me, interconnected with invisible string.

Yes, but up at the pond behind the house there are some pretty primitive spectacles. I was in the canoe yesterday, way back in the part of the pond I would never swim in because back there the place creams with life. Take the filmy blobs that hang on the surface. I think they are tadpole beginnings or fish eggs. The floating jelly snots bubble with single-cell DNA, hinged to the water like something you might see in an intergalactic photograph: flows of gaseous life, a mess of substance until, what? – it boils into a planet or a star or a frog? See what I mean? It's easy out here to start having ideas about breathing protozoan being the glue and all of us as part of the same atomic muck. Oh, and lately I've seen things flit by out of the corner of my eye. The other evening I thought I saw my now deceased ex mother-in-law, Marion, pass by the kitchen window. I was outside and she would have walked by the sink. I probably shouldn't have mentioned that.

In the Bible, Moses talked to a burning bush, but it could have been a tree. Maybe my tree and I are meant to form a new sect? Unfortunately, I always come to the same stark dilemma with regard to the organized beliefs of the world: I can't do it. Not an ounce of comfort either if that's the purpose. I have dealt with death: my dear father's demise early in life. I've been sick, one time dangerously so. I married a man who dissolved into my evil other, and not once in any of those instances did I think of surrendering my pain to an icon. Time passed, I healed. Studying the mind doesn't help either because this complex piece of machinery, the human brain, can have so much go wrong with it, and we have no clue yet why it is here in the first place. Evolution? Some disallow it, preferring an anonymous genius at work. What about those who suffer the developmental disorder I am researching? They are assumed to be lost, but I am not so sure.

I'm losing my focus. You might be wondering what wisdom the tree imparted. It certainly didn't offer advice on this paper I'm supposed to be writing. I didn't mean just now to cast the tree in a lesser light. Who could hate a tree? Suburban developers, big box stores; farmers find them inconvenient or profitable to slice. I have a friend who told me that one day when he was a kid his father chopped down all the trees in their yard. Big old trees. Maybe he'd grown fed up raking their leaves each autumn. Anyway, he later regretted what he'd done but never explained why.

Marion (my ex mother-in-law) once hid my teapot. I have never been chipper in the morning; the utter fatigue of waking up is a trial. Neurologists tell us the mind never sleeps, is always tooling around, sorting through its biology, picking up bytes from the surrounding night – if only from the bedclothes or the pillow texture – always on, like a private city. Only coma and anesthesia shut the conscious process down, and even then minute stimuli still excite the organism.

"We should have John cut another swath to the pond," Marion said, looking out of the window that morning of the teapot. "The wild turkeys will eat all the blueberries."

I was silently searching for the teapot that had mysteriously left the place where I normally kept it.

"What do you think? A second path to the pond?"

"The turkeys have no supermarkets, Marion; they are

welcome to the blueberries," I said.

"You don't like blueberries?"

"I love blueberries."

"What on earth are you looking for?"

"The teapot. Have you seen it?"

"Oh, that. I put it in the dining room. No one drinks tea."

My father was British; I come from a long line of tea drinkers. I cannot have a day without my tea. How did my husband's mother fail to know this? I shuffled to the dining room. "Marion?" I called out weakly, "where in the dining room?"

"What?" Marion called from the kitchen. "Oh, I couldn't find where it went so I stuck it in the liquor cabinet."

I found the pot tucked among the martini glasses and cocktail napkins. "Marion," I remember saying, "I'm a tea drinker."

To which she replied, "Well, you grew up here and should drink as Americans do." That may have led to the first true moment of communion between me and the tree that spoke. I retreated from Marion to the pentagon room, to drink my tea among the harmonious offerings of nature . . .

I'm sorry, my phone rang. It was nothing; I ought to have let the machine get it. Trivial, what the man on the other end wanted. A dinner date, if you must know. I declined. The man comes up on weekends and disturbs me with his massive logic and financial success. I would rather talk to the tree. Really, after my initial fright I felt quite at home with the greenery talking.

You are probably concluding I am mad, passing up a free dinner with a nice guy. I could share the story of the talking tree, get it off my chest. But, did I say he was nice? And I'm not certain he would pay for dinner, though he probably would, and then expect to see how my panties look lying on the floor at the foot of his bed. He tries to impress, but he speaks nasally and is self-important. My caretaker, George, has warned me, Marshall – that's the man's name – has designs on my property.

Another thing about the mentally disordered people in my study is they lack spite. The obverse is also true: joy, empathy, kindness, tenderness – you get the idea – not functioning. A handicap when it comes to conceiving an idea of the world, or the self, to bridging the chasm between one person and another.

I think it was the Queen Anne's lace that opened me to nature's voice. We'd had a late start getting back to the city that Sunday. John was in a rage; the traffic would be murder on the West Side. I'd wanted to pick a bouquet of Queen Anne's lace to take back. They were bobbing and waving like little Breton caps in the breeze, beckoning me into the field. I thought they were sighing like grandmothers in lacy white hats. John – my husband still – told me to get into the car. "We can buy a dozen lilies in town," he said. "Those fucking things," he yelled, "are just a bunch of stinking weeds." Call it a turning point.

The tree actually said very little. I hope you don't feel cheated. Was it not enough that a tree spoke? Did it have to tell me some deep secret, one science will never unravel? The tree spoke and nothing changed. It was a simple communication on a rainy afternoon.

Drops were falling from the ends of the tree's tender green tips. The fragment that spoke seemed to lean in, to move towards me behind the glass. That's what caused the initial fright, seeing it lean in ever so slightly like that to tell me it was standing in the rain, which, frankly, I could see for myself. It told me that it always stood: in the cold of winter and through storms, the dry of summer, heat of day and dark of night. I suddenly understood a tree stands its whole life. I'd wanted to ask what it thought of birds among its branches, or the diminishing rain forests and other majestic amputations. It might have enlightened me regarding any number of questions. Did it know about the Kyoto Protocol? It might have gotten in a mood, had a few choice words to say about all the houses, furniture, toilet paper, ships and wooden legs mankind has made over the millennia. Supposing it had called out to the forest that edges the clearing, stirred up malevolent whisperings among the thousands of trees surrounding me? But no, the cold summer rain continued to fall, and I have heard nothing more from the tree.

I'd like to go for a walk outside, touch the thick bark of that very wet tree, only we are not equipped for the rain, you and I, as a tree is, so I'll settle for a pot of tea by the window, a cup of *Lapsang Souchong*. You decide for yourself if I'm crazy or not; if a tree can speak or not. I would only suggest listening for yourself.

Spirals Around Two Peaks

Anne Whitehouse

Over the planet vast migrations are occurring. By the sounds he knows what he cannot see with his little eyes: immense sheets of ice are cracking, and all the water in the world is rising, tumbling. It curls down rocks, it roars. In the deep lakes fish in their first, larval stage are leaving the shingle beds where their eggs were laid. What they know of life is a journey they did not begin; they are carried by a current, propelled by a wind they cannot conceive of. Everything moves before them but the fixed rock and its silky mantle of sand. He does not know how they sense direction and stem the current, how they decide on their own way. The rivers rise, the world expands its levels, and flocks of birds are flying to nest. Herds move across the plains, and in the forests insects slowly unfurl their thin legs. Trailing their calves, singing their eerie songs, the whales swim to the distant poles.

He is dreamy and disconsolate, and the world, which tendered invitations to the landlocked boy, now at the last gate, at the continent's edge, denies him. Did he misread the signals? He remembers the stiff dead under their white sheets and the screech of the wheels as he rolled them down fluorescent-lit corridors. It was neither night nor day. Like Charon poling his ferry, he accepted payment for his service. The creamy concrete walls, the echoing linoleum, the overhead light suspended from a cracking ceiling were all he saw of roads, but he knew what others shunned: life's last ignominy before ceding to death. The care he gave was useless, but giving flowed from him like an endless wave. Yet the sea, rising, would fall; at last he retreated.

He took little with him. (Name the ways in which less is more.) His driving was intent but capricious; sometimes he stopped by a yellow field and got out to feel the emptiness of the sky. But the towns he passed were changing; they no longer faced the land but grew towards each other, always more alike. They imported their buildings ready-made just as they imported their citizens: they still believed in growth. These people he glimpsed through the windshields of other cars and overheard at breakfast in diners had a pink, indoor look; their bones seemed already softened as if they were dissolving, internally. They had never thought of being forgotten.

Like the others they had come to claim possession. The land hid things they hoped to detect with their shiny instruments and extract with the powerful machines they had brought with them, for the rock was so hard and deep that only an immense force could break it. Safely distant, they pushed the controls that ignited explosions. An orange flare lit the sky. He left the landscape being laid to waste and drove towards the mountains they could not yet topple.

There could be no reconciliation. An ache grew inside his nostrils when he saw the ranging peaks as if he were already inhaling their cold glitter. He had read the accounts of others who had been moved by the eternal snows. He imagined discovering at the foot of an uneasy pyramid of boulders an alpine columbine, tiny, deep-blue spurs ringing its white cup: he admired the blossoms whose miniature perfection was confined to mountains. He was seeking an inaccessible place.

Of what was his solitude? He was a restless outpost, recovering what his kind had nearly lost. He left his car parked and locked; with a backpack and walking stick he climbed trails. He heard the aspen's rattle and the hollow spruce; fatigue weighted his legs. At times he thought he was ill: his bones ached, his throat was raw; hard lumps swelled the glands of his neck. His body felt hot, dry, and tight. He pitched his tent beside a glacial lake that mirrored the moon, crawled in, and slept. He dreamed of fish under winter ice. When he awoke it was night, but the moon was gone. Standing in the short, still grass, he divided the stars into the constellations an ancient, sea-going people had invented. Consciously he felt his pulse's definite beat, and he blessed his life whose existence he had at times disputed. In the morning he was lighter, clearer. On his little stove he brewed tea from herbs; he heard the bleating of sheep far off, a herd let loose to feed in summer. Below the clouds blown in at dawn, the light was shadowless. From the snowmelt lake he filled his flask and consulted his map for the land's features.

As he walked, he felt stronger. It was as if he emanated a power. Only a secret knowledge could free him from the need to claim what he could touch with his two hands. It meant being able to watch from many places at once, being able to locate points of vantage. A light rain wet him; the clouds rolled back; and the meadow changed under the bright brief glare of the sun that threw it into relief, forced it to contrast. But this too was ephemeral, would pass and return. What was hidden was not lost.

After four days he returned. His food was almost gone. He did not pretend to be a frontiersman; he was not in his natural home. All he physically needed he had brought with him, except for the water. He was technologically equipped for a reclaimed wilderness where the animals were suffered to let roam. Still, they had kept their shyness. In his sojourn he had seen no living creature but birds and the flickering shadows of fish in lake water, yet he was surrounded by so much space. He stood at the continental divide. If he spilled his water in a clear sluice, the trickles would seep into the ground and separate. Opposite each other, two oceans immense, blind, and dark. The wind ruffled his hair and the short grass. From here any direction was a turning back.

~

The land slips away steeply below him; it is touched down the length of its long coast by the deeper ocean. He is at the apex of another vision. A city, beautiful and clean, climbs up and down the hills. He looks past it a long way into the water. He hopes that the specks he sees far-off are animals frolicking, but he thinks they are not. This is how he used to feel when he walked through silent, sunny rooms, hearing uncertain thuds coming from, he knew, a nearby house under construction. The cat spoke to itself; outside the branches were quivering in a wind that rolled past the storm windows its bright dust of snow. Inside plants grew, green, silent, and sealed, and the wooden floor answered the tap of his heels.

Now he resides in a sunset land of mild and misty winters. He lives in endings: the long afternoons of eucalyptus barely rustling outside the window, of wisteria hanging fragrant and thicker than grapes. His pen scratches over the tedious forms he must complete, one after another, collecting facts through interrogation, listening for lies, bargaining hypothetical money for lost wealth. He is always encountering strangers.

In going, did he mean to leave or to arrive? He wonders

about the original explorers who, as the emissaries of governments, possessed and divided. As they rowed down a river in the morning mist or stumbled over jagged rocks or stood in the shaded, primeval forest, did they fear the emptying of the world's stores? They were the first and last witnesses of earthly perfection. When they lay coughing and dying in the rumpled sheets, shut off in some shuttered room, which was stronger in them, the glint of the gold crucifix on the darkened wall or the shadowless breath of a pearly morning?

Both visions pass before him, and then he sees himself writing out the checks. He has been taught how to compute risk for the forms. Were the explorers insured? He does not have to believe in what he does to perform his duties. When, over a glass-topped desk, he speaks the language of gain and loss, part of him separates and stands off, immune, like the nodding green in the window. He admires the lush, indifferent beauty of this sunset land, the hedges of dense bougainvillea, the spiny stems concealed by blossoms. And still the tiny alpine flowers were not less loved.

Patience sits quietly, patience must watch. People throng the streets at five p.m.; the traffic clusters under a strange falling light that slants and glitters across the white spires, but leaves the grey, fog-bound sky untouched. In small parks, on benches painted as red as Chinese lacquer, old people sit closely, reading and musing in the last daylight.

All the people in the streets are not commuters. Many are visitors, come to see and to exclaim over a charm generally recognized and preserved. Views are its delight, a secluded green nook in a hill's irregularity an agreeable surprise. But all do not hunger after the same sights. There are whole quarters for tourists mainly, who may not realize that what they visit has been transformed by their presence: boutiques lodged in corners of an old factory, craft vendors who also once were tourists and remained. The vendors set up their cases on a wharf that only sees foot traffic now. What they sell is attractive and well-made: wooden boxes carefully jointed, silver pendants, faceted crystals that flash like fire. These lovely trinkets are not always the work of their own hand; indeed, some have come from distant continents to be sold here.

Still, there is much, he knows, that is native under the gloss. From the specked, glinting horizon, the wind rolls in to his windy hilltop, salty, with a hint of the spices cargoed by a vanished ship. This is no beach resort; the water is cold and the air often chilly; he could walk all day in the grey, green-tinged mist and keep the feeling he was arriving at the end of something. He still does not know quite what it was he was seeking or what it meant when he stood on the rounded peak of the other mountain and all that fell away from him was division. Before, orderly, antiseptic, he dispensed the dead; now he dispenses payment for damaged property whose ruin, the owner must prove, was accidental. In the end, his allegiance is to chance, a no which might turn to yes in mid-utterance, a dolphin surfacing at the edge of his vision. Once he thought he was looking for a home, and still, when he sees an old man watering his alley flowerpots or a father unfurling a kite for his child, he feels a twinge for what he fears he'll never have.

But he is never forlorn in the mornings, driving through the east bay towns with their little stucco houses whose colors recall the faded gaudiness of the tropics and their humble architecture. For a while he can drive aimlessly; he can pretend he has nowhere in particular to go, though a client waits in a numbered house in a street named Adeline or San Leandro. These places are too new to have been abandoned. The same green waves, but the fog rarely comes this far, and the days are sunny.

On a corner lot, a burned-out grocery, boarded-up. The lines in its neon sign are twisted; its facade is blackened by smoke. An acrid, leathery smell still lives in it among the hidden wreckage of shelves and machines that only the starlings see, alighting from the gaping roof. Already posters have been glued to the plywood boards nailed onto the window frames. Later he will examine inventories of what was lost; now the store is just a general eyesore on a small-town street. Two children pass on a tricycle, one sitting and pedaling, the other standing on the metal shelf between the rolling back wheels. They are absorbed; they do not worry where their mother will shop now the store is gone. For a brief moment they steer past him, shrill and clattering. Then the street is quiet. He is far from where adults spend their days.

Waiting for a tardy proprietor at a sleepy, mid-morning crossroads, he begins to feel, as present as the seasonless, eternal sun on his back, the difference wrought in him. He has achieved less than exploration, more than a change of climate. Someday he will leave the California claims adjustor like empty snakeskin, desiccated to an impossible thinness, blown across dry dirt.

In between that time-to-be and this, a succession of mimetic days. Change is in the drive over the bridge. For adventure he stands, binoculars in hand, protected by wool and Gore-Tex, in an open boat on grey, tipping waters. Others are with him on this excursion. On the way out they chat with each other, trading facts, while he watches the water, and this is why he is the first to see the smooth hump barely surfacing, immense, turning as the world must turn. The water pours off seamless skin in a thin, clear fall, and ripples out, and finally the foam dissolves.

The horizon also is water, and the clouds there low and scudding, but over his head it is clear. He is prepared – warm, his lens in focus, yet nothing else breaks the water but its own solitary, pointless waves occasionally stirred by wind.

The moments he wears close are serendipitous: he is walking hunched forward in a soft, spring rain; from an alley quickly passed by, a smell of laundry, and the low fog curls at his feet like a living creature. The little shops have rolled out their awnings; he has come to buy fresh bread, milk, honey. Before he reaches home, the bag will be wet and tattering. He will eat and watch the raindrops slide off the window.

Snug and warm in the rainy morning, his mind holds a memory like a breath its warm mist. His room's walls are white; he is curled on the couch in a knitted afghan of alpaca wool. Its browns and blacks chime against the place in his mind he is entering, slowly, creeping at the vague edge of a park. He walks on wet, flat stones; he crosses a bridge over gurgling water and passes under a gate; the paved avenue before him is lined by low buildings and locked yards. Before he saw it, he smelled it.

In one of the cramped outdoor cages of this city zoo, half a dozen bighorn sheep crowd against the small diamonds of a chain-linked fence. An eye flattened against smooth, light-brown fur fills a single segment. The horns curve thick and spiraling, their heaviness weights the head back, arching the neck. He had longed to see these animals in the mountains, yet he had neither spied them in a craggy fastness nor a meadow starred with flowers. The captured animals are being fed by aged women whom he sees from the back of their scarf-covered heads and worn cloth coats; below the unthreading hemlines, their muscled calves are knobby. He does not have to hear them speak to know they have come from an unlucky part of the world. Their fingers thrust leaves of ice-green lettuce past the fence to the sheep's masticating lips. The lettuce is in a moisture-lined plastic bag that is slowly unplumping. The sheep's incisors take the lacy leaves silently, their lips suck softly, funneling in their salad as if it were an inhaled breath. It occurs to him that this is all these women will ever see of the wild. When they sense him, they change: they mutter as they snatch the lettuce from the bag; their eyes dart at him to keep away. Still, he watches for a while, his hands clasped behind his back, before he leaves by the wrought-iron gate.

Outside, on the sandy path, the eucalyptus trees are waving up and down, dark green with silvery insides. He hears them fluttering like the wings of tiny birds. Both wavering and fixed, each leaf is a green, articulate tip that speaks to him, the listener. Down the path, past large, splashy flowers that cradle the mist, he might take any man for a ghost. A long promenade ending in a cliff's edge and far below, a meager strip of beach. In a cove, the sea's magnified echo, driftwood, and the various, thick kelps plaited together, pea-green, fuchsia, black. He enjoys expecting what will lie just before his advance and delights in uncertain coincidence. Out of small choices, he shapes his life.

He glimpses a man half-sidled behind a tree, his hands burrowed in his pants pockets. He lets the man slide away to a faint menace as he propels himself forward, swift and controlled, without a glance back. Up the rise and over, and something light hits the ground just behind him. He curbs a wish to flee; a quick turn shows him the hurled branch, the retrieving dog, the genial, ambling owner. Then the other man is lost to him behind pale fog; he takes the stick, and the rough edges of the dog's eager bark fold into each other.

Remembering, he sips the last of his lukewarm drink in his safe room, the soft afghan over his knees. The man who stood on the mountain is already distant; the hospital's man is blessedly laid to rest. The sea curls and straightens, wrinkled by rain; the boats are lashed to the marina, and he dozes on the sofa. Not often does he allow himself frittered mornings. He stretches, and his elbow tips the coffee dregs on his afghan; the liquid stands in drops on the wool. The accident rouses him; he gently rinses the soiled corner and hangs it over the shower rod to dry. The smell of the animal fills the bathroom, travels into the hallway. Tiny hairs fluff out from the nap as if they still protected living flesh.

And now he is restless. His wooden floors shine as if something might surface in them; a table's wavy leg extends like an uncoiling rope into a depth he cannot touch. Something lives down there past the grain, forever removed from him, a shape melding into another. To notice them fuse and evolve is to develop another kind of vision, as if one were watching flat spaces out to sea, islands of indigo blue gently bobbing on green, surface blooms attached to a stem, nets of microscopic plankton. Out from the shore, in a motorboat belonging to another man, he will sit in a pile of life preservers, slipping a black rubber fin over his ankle. In a wetsuit, he will strap on tank and belt, adjust the mask, put the regulator in his mouth, and slip awkwardly from the anchored, tipping boat into the water.

He will learn how to propel himself downward. As the depth of water grows between him and the open air, he will pant nervously, sucking in large quantities of the oxygen strapped to his back. A stream of bubbles will cascade behind him. He had not thought the ocean was so full of sounds. He will hear something hollow like a waterfall, the vibration of a taut wire, and echoes pushing like little fists. His experienced partner beckons and he follows. His breaths no longer dig into him; his heartbeat eases; fear uncoils from him as he commences something new.

The wind is always moving: a bronze ruffle down the yellow wheat, a warm current in a cold sea, the scrub oak battened to the mountain. Navigated by birds, bearing weather and sound and the weightless seeds of plants, wind is blowing across continents, over oceans. By what it brings, he knows it. In the hesitant drip from the waves, he perceives at once vast plains, a satiny petal teared by rain. Puddles grow in low places. He retains a dampness, a residue, like the animal smell of alpaca wool. Once, as he lay, a sleeping child, a shining light was flicked in his face quickly, just to check, and taken away. The man recalls how the child, startled awake in his own bedroom from which the intruder had already retreated, saw, superimposed on the customary darkness, a chorus of spotlights slowly growing grainy and dissolving, and how, later, the boy remained stunned by what had already disappeared from his vision.

~

People do not seem to realize that their opinion of the world
is also a confession of their character. — Emerson

Annual Migration

Patty Somlo

Aunt Marta rocked in a wobbly wooden chair on the front porch. Pinpoints of starlight dazzled the darkness all around. Aunt Marta's sisters, Berta and Maria Luz, were complaining, as usual, about their husbands. The same dissatisfied tune those sisters never grew tired of singing.

Except, now, Aunt Marta said something new.

"It's almost time for the butterflies."

~

The following Saturday night, Aunt Marta shook her nephew Gilberto awake.

"It's time, *mi hijo*. It's time."

Gilberto rolled over, pushed himself up to a sitting position and let his legs dangle from the bed while he rubbed his eyes.

"Where are we going, Auntie?" the boy asked, wishing he could crawl back under the sheet and resume his dreaming.

"You will see," his aunt said. "Hurry up now and get dressed."

Gilberto buttoned his shirt, pulled on his pants and slipped on his sandals. Aunt Marta said, "Let's go, Gilberto."

Marta grabbed Gilberto's hand after he stepped out the front door. In her other hand, she was lugging a heavy iron pot.

The pathway below the porch steps was dusty and dry. No lights were on. A nearly full moon lit up the path as they walked.

Gilberto, who suddenly realized he was hungry, breathed in the aroma of beans and rice coming from Aunt Marta's pot. The mountain air was cool and dry.

Before long, Gilberto saw flickering lights. The boy felt less afraid. Light from burning candles broke through the dark, along with the white glare of several flashlights.

A man was singing and strumming a guitar. Women, a few old men and kids were sitting on bright blue, red and green blankets, next to small gray stones stuck in the ground. They had plates of food laid out.

Aunt Marta led Gilberto to where his aunts, cousins and several old great uncles were gathered. Marta set her pot down next to other pots and bowls and plates filled with stew and pozole, rice, beans, corn tortillas, and mango slices.

As soon as they had settled themselves, Marta tapped Gilberto's Great Uncle Dagberto on the arm.

"Uncle," she whispered. "Will you tell us a story?"

Uncle Dagberto shook his head, as if he'd just woken up. He gave the assembled family a shy smile. His gums were pink and naked where his bottom teeth should have been. This caused him to whistle, softly, as the words slipped through his lips.

"On this night," Uncle Dagberto began, "we come to honor our ancestors. Every year, they come back."

He tried to catch the children's eyes. Once he did, almost in a whisper, he said, "Our ancestors come in the form of beautiful butterflies."

In the secret way of a quiet, shy child, Gilberto decided that the butterflies were his mama and papa. He had been praying for their return for a long time.

Uncle Dagberto neglected to tell a part of the story, so Aunt Marta decided to fill it in.

"The butterflies used to come every year," she said. "Every year on this day. But now they do not come sometimes. And when they come, there are so very few."

Aunt Marta had one more thing to say.

"Every year, more and more butterflies die. Without the trees to keep them warm, those beautiful butterflies cannot survive."

~

At first, letters came from Gilberto's mother smelling of roses. She promised to visit, and also said she'd send for Gilberto, to come live with her in the United States.

A decade went by, and neither Gilberto's mother nor his father returned. Though he still called her Auntie, Gilberto now considered Marta his mother. The years had gone by without a visit or an invitation for Gilberto to go live in the United States. Only envelopes arrived, full of dollars for Aunt Marta.

When Gilberto turned eleven, the envelopes filled with dollars even stopped. He stopped waiting for his mother and father to come back.

A few months after Gilberto's seventeenth birthday, he gathered at the cemetery with his aunts, cousins and the few old uncles still living in Anguenguero. As the family did every October, they were waiting for the butterflies to return. Gilberto understood now that the butterflies were not his mama and papa. They weren't some old ancestors either.

What Gilberto wanted was money – enough to buy a big, shiny American car. A car that would help him escape from his sleepy town.

~

Gilberto carried his boots as he tiptoed through the dark house. He didn't want to run into a chair or a table in the two small crowded rooms and wake up his aunt.

He met the other men, Javier and Jaime, at the north edge of town, where the paved road stopped. Lights from their cigarettes glowed in the dark.

"We have to be careful," Javier warned.

Gilberto and the two other men had heard the government was paying local people to guard the trees. Just the night before, Aunt Marta had told Gilberto that two men from the neighboring village were killed by a gang that made money selling wood from trees the government workers were trying to protect. Gilberto knew Aunt Marta was on the side of the pansies who wanted to save the trees, so butterflies would have a place to sleep. He'd been tempted to ask his aunt, "Why is it more important to save butterflies than to make money for ourselves?"

Javier walked at the front, followed by Jaime, with Gilberto bringing up the rear. Suddenly, Javier stopped.

It took several minutes for Gilberto to see what had caught Javier's attention. Flashlights flickered on and off. The area all around the tree trunks was lit up. Gilberto could see a group of people standing guard.

~

The next afternoon, Gilberto was walking toward the center of the plaza. He was glad that he, Javier and Jaime had made it out of the forest without being spotted. But since they weren't able to cut down a single tree, he wasn't a bit closer to his dream of having a car that would take him out of Anguenguero.

He'd forgotten that it was October, when Anguenguero got crowded with tourists who came to see the butterflies arrive. He stepped across the plaza through the crowd on his way to the little store.

"Ow," he heard and jumped back, startled.

"You stepped on my toe," the young woman said to him, but he didn't understand, since she'd said the words in English. She looked up then and told him the same thing in Spanish.

Gilberto noticed that the young woman's hair was the color of ripe corn. Thick strands blew in the wind and brushed her shoulders.

Without thinking, Gilberto moved closer.

"I am sorry," he said, not able to take his eyes off the woman's face. She was staring at him with the most beautiful green eyes.

"Have you come to wait for the butterflies?" she asked now.

Gilberto wanted to say whatever would make this angelic creature smile.

"*Sí*," he said, a little breathless.

She told him her name was Lisa and said she had come all the way from Washington, where the constant rain made the landscape green and created powerful, rushing waterfalls. She studied butterflies at the university and had come to Anguenguero to witness the end of their miraculous annual migration.

"Did you know they sometimes fly fifty miles a day on their journey here from Canada?"

Gilberto had never heard such a thing. Neither did he know the amount of land a butterfly – or, for that matter, a man – could pass in fifty miles. If she had said a million miles, it would not have made any more sense, since Gilberto had only attended school up to the third grade.

"I did not know," Gilberto said, unable to take his eyes off Lisa's heart-shaped face.

"There used to be about a hundred and fifty million of them that migrated here every year," she said, her eyes wide, as she shook her head and smiled. "Can you imagine? A hundred and fifty million butterflies filling the sky?"

Gilberto couldn't imagine a number of butterflies beyond twenty, since that's as high as he could count. He wanted to impress this beautiful girl, but what could he say? He knew almost nothing of the butterflies. Worse still, he knew almost nothing about every single thing in the world.

Except one. He recalled the story his Great Uncle Dagberto had told when he was a small boy.

Before he had a chance to talk, Lisa went on.

"The butterflies couldn't survive the winter here, when the trees started to be chopped down," she said. "Less and less of them mated and less and less of their offspring made it back to Canada. Everyone began to worry that the butterflies would soon be extinct."

Gilberto did not know the meaning of "extinct," even though she had said it in Spanish.

"Everyone must do their part to save the trees," she added.

91

At that moment, her fingers pressed against Gilberto's skin. His right forearm tingled.

"Men are cutting the trees down for money. We are here to keep watch, to save the trees and the butterflies."

Gilberto was surprised how different those words sounded, coming from a green-eyed angel. He did not feel the urge to argue that people needed to survive more than butterflies. Instead, he wanted her to know that he agreed and to impress her with his own special knowledge.

"When I was a little boy," he began, looking off into the distance, as if his childhood waited for him there, "we used to sit in the cemetery and wait for the butterflies each year."

He told Lisa about the beans and rice his Aunt Marta carried in the pot and how, the first time, he did not know where they were going. And then, as the words spilled out, the story took an unexpected turn.

"I thought the butterflies were my mother and father," he said.

Lisa suggested that they take a seat on one of the benches surrounding the plaza. Gilberto followed, but his mind was back in that time. He pictured his mother's face, so close he could have run his fingers over her smile. She continued smiling, as she brushed the hair from his eyes.

"You must have been very sad," Gilberto heard Lisa say now. "You must have missed your parents a lot."

"I did," he said, though he had never before admitted this to anyone.

"Then I stopped thinking about them. I pushed them out of my mind."

Lisa rested her hand on top of Gilberto's. The sky suddenly grew dark.

~

The first butterfly landed on Gilberto's shoulder. The second one alighted on his head.

Lisa cried out the moment a wing brushed her arm.

"They're back," she shouted.

Before long, Gilberto was covered with butterflies. Velvety black and yellow wings formed a protective layer over Lisa's pale skin. Butterflies crowded onto her cheeks.

Unable to control himself, Gilberto started to giggle. Moments later, Lisa joined in.

Gilberto leaned over and kissed that girl. She was draped in a coat of velvet wings, along with him.

~

While civilization has been improving our houses,
it has not equally improved the people
who are to inhabit them. – Thoreau

To Zanzibar

Rivka Keren

Translated from Hebrew by Dalit Shmueli

Thirty years I was married to a woman I did not love, and when she became ill and died, my world fell apart. I was left trapped within myself like a tortoise in its shell, or in the words of my Hungarian ancestors, like a frog in a bucket. I became a recluse. I fasted. I lost my will to start the day. The familiar routine that I had taken for granted was gone forever. I comforted myself with the thought that in any case my life was drifting towards its end. Does it really matter if you go alone or together? I started to wonder.

Beneath the stone arches of an old Arab house on Yefet Street in Jaffa, I ran a spice import business that I had inherited from my family. My father had started out by selling paprika and over time contacted other spice merchants, corresponded with them and expanded the business. Friends from the nearby flea market would come over for coffee, bringing baklava, and turned the place into a Tower of Babel. Turkish, Persian, Bulgarian, Rumanian, Arabic, Hungarian, Ladino . . .

Something of each language stuck to me, like the smell of the spices I had helped to weigh, pack, and sell since early childhood. My mother wanted me to study medicine, so she wouldn't have to go to doctors, but I was more attracted to the Liberal Arts. Here and there I wrote a short story, a play, and dozens of poems. I never published anything. My father led me to understand that as an only child, the fate of the business lay on my shoulders. I traveled to London for a two year apprenticeship with Mr. Caesar, an acquaintance of my father and a veteran spice merchant, who had diversified his business. There, in England, my eyes were opened. Mr. Caesar was not a big talker, I would even say that he was unusually secretive about his personal life, but he had a fascinating collection of travel books that aroused in me a sudden desire to leave everything and take off.

Of course, I didn't do that. Next door to my shop in Jaffa was a mattress factory owned by two Hungarian brothers who had been like family to me since I was a child. When I returned home they invited me to spend Sabbaths with them, consoled me over the tragic death of my mother, who had been run over on her way to the neurologist on Zamenhof Street, and after a while they introduced me to my wife.

Looking back I know we led a comfortable life. My business provided us with a decent living. We got through all the wars safely. After my father died, we settled in the apartment I grew up in which was close to the sea, and was overly spacious because we had no children. As was the apartment, so were our friends inherited from my father. They were elderly, told the same jokes over and over, spoke fondly of their aches and pains, and cursed the politicians in a multitude of languages. Amid the bustle my wife was a contemplative woman. Sometimes she would focus on one spot for a long while and think. She helped out a lot in the shop and excelled in knitting and sewing but developed an allergy to cinnamon, suffering bouts of coughing and migraines until finally I suggested that she stay at home. I realized that spices made her unwell. She received medication and allergy shots and all kinds of alternative therapies and nothing helped. I am allergic to life, she once said, and that sentence troubled me because I could not refute it. In the end she closeted herself in the bedroom and never went out again.

Left alone, I began to think that there was something that I had wanted to say to my wife, but now it was too late. It was summer. The smell of fish and watermelon was in the air. What was it that I had wanted to say to her? I would walk along the beach until I reached Park Haatzmaut and return home with no answers. Suddenly I had two keys. An empty refrigerator. Useless objects. My life fell into a new kind of routine. After the initial nausea and forced silences, I felt that I was starting to get used to it.

Previously, there had been hope for some kind of change, hope that I secretly preferred over the change itself, because expectations expanded the future while the actual change might diminish it. Now there were no expectations left as far as I was concerned, and I felt relieved. I am free of the burden of change, I said to myself. This unfamiliar loneliness is the only change I have been condemned to, and I have no right to complain. So I thought. And then, one evening, Mr. Caesar phoned. He expressed his condolences, reminded me of his visits to Israel and the years that I had spent with him, and asked me to come urgently to London. He said that my trip would be mutually beneficial. For decades we had kept up a strictly business-like relationship, and I couldn't say that I knew him well. He told me that he had a large spice trade business in Zanzibar, something that I only vaguely knew about, like all his other business dealings, and that he wanted

me to supervise until the new manager came to the island. He
added that he couldn't think of anyone more suitable than me,
and in any case, it was only temporary. Moses, do this for me,
he said. Come to London first; I'll take care of all the
necessary documents and travel arrangements. Think about it
and give me your answer in the morning.

Our conversation made me feel uneasy. Contrary to how I
had felt in my youth, I no longer wanted to travel anywhere,
least of all to Africa. I spent the night in a conflict, with the
intention of finding a way to avoid this imposition without
offending the good Mr. Caesar, who had taught me most of
what I knew about spices and medicinal herbs. I asked myself,
why me. Why now. And why Zanzibar. If I had known then
what I know today, it would have been much easier to make a
decision. But few have the gift of prophecy, and I was but a
sixty year old widower from Jaffa lacking prophetic skills.

In the morning, I called Mr. Caesar and told him I would
come and talk to him. He sounded pleased. I rented out my
shop to a Persian acquaintance and went to London. The city
was veiled in fog like the new circumstances of my life and it
poured for three days.

It always rains here, I said.

Not always, said Mr. Caesar. Sometimes the sun shines,
have you forgotten?

We drank tea by the fireplace. Mr. Caesar had shrunk
somewhat, but his eyes had kept their sparkle. He wore a gold
ring inlaid with a ruby. On his visits to Jaffa he had become
close to my wife, maybe by virtue of her minimalistic manner
of expression, and now I had to go over all the details of her
illness.

She was a special woman, said Mr. Caesar. Your father was

special too.

He repeated the word special and said that I had to leave for Stone Town as soon as possible.

It *is* a special place, he said. His gaze came to rest on my neck. That Hamsa charm you are wearing, that was your wife's.

I was surprised that he remembered and admitted that after giving my wife's clothes to charity, I had saved her favorite pendant.

She thought that it would bring us luck, I said.

Luck is like an uninvited guest, said Mr. Caesar; it appears with no prior notice.

~

Within a few days I was given an envelope with a visa, a work permit, and a stamped immunization card. The answers to my questions were brief and inadequate.

Your worries are unnecessary, said Mr. Caesar firmly. He put a jar of anti-malaria pills into my hand. Check the expiration date, he said. You won't need them, but just in case.

I told him that I had to be back in Jaffa by spring at the latest, but my old friend hushed me.

Spring is far away . . . in Zanzibar it rains in the spring . . . everything has its time . . . mention my name if there are any problems.

And so I arrived in Dar es-Salaam on a direct flight from London, armed only with my fears and with partial information. I kept my distance from beggars, street peddlers, pickpockets, and prostitutes, as Mr. Caesar had advised. I hid most of my money in my socks. The ferry to the island was crowded with chickens, goats, and other domestic animals, and all the passengers were local peasants except for one freckle-faced backpacker and a couple of middle-aged tourists who tried to make eye contact with me. I stood against the railing and hoped that the ferry wouldn't sink. The sea was clear and calm and different from the sea I was familiar with. Suddenly I was enveloped by the strong fragrance of cloves. I had never been to the far-off places that my spices came from, but the dense strip of coconut trees on the beach, the fishing boats in the blue water and the vibrant bustle on the pier matched the images in my mind. Mr. Caesar's name did indeed hasten the bureaucracy. A man of a different temperament than mine would probably have felt as if in a brightly colored postcard, and taken endless pictures, like the tourists who had arrived with me. I was tired, sweaty and all I wanted was to shower and sleep.

I put on sunglasses and made my way between the many street peddlers selling bus and ferry tickets and swarms of children that followed me speaking Swahili and garbled English, pushing their wares in front of me. I succumbed and bought some candy made of coconut flakes that reminded me of the pink coconut candy they used to sell at the movie theater when I was a child. I finally extricated myself from the annoying crowd and walked toward the alleyways of Stone Town. My suitcase was light. I had only come for several months to a tropical climate, and I had brought nothing but cotton clothing, medications, and some books. It took me a long time to find the address. Mr. Caesar's warehouse was in a fortress-like building, which boasted a massive, brass-studded wooden gate. The woman who lived on the upper floor, I was told, was called Lilliana, and she was supposed to take care of my every need and transfer supervision of the warehouse to me until the manager from India arrived.

She is a very *special* woman, Mr. Caesar had said, in a tone that reverberated in my head as a warning. I knocked at the door using the elephant-shaped knocker. It was dusk and orange seagulls were circling above. A veiled woman peeked from a neighboring house.

The muezzin called to prayer. The aroma of cloves was driving me wild.

I heard the sound of English being spoken and someone walking down a flight of stairs. The rusty hinges and lock creaked, and in the doorway stood a very thin woman with theatrical make-up, wrapped in a red tunic with gold stripes and wearing a long flowing blond wig. She wore beach sandals and turquoise beads. I was so surprised that I froze in place, but my hostess shook my hand firmly and introduced herself with an amused smile, as one who knows the effect her appearance has on people.

You are Moses; Mr. Caesar told me about you. Welcome to Zanzibar.

She walked me past the dimly lit hallway into a green garden, with a water basin in the center, a peacock and two magnificent parrots. Cats napped in every corner. I could hear a distant drumming. Brass bells chimed in the wind. Lilliana called to a young black child named Culpa, and he carried my belongings to the second floor.

What do you think of our place? Lilliana asked.

I don't know yet, I replied.

You are tired and you want to shower and sleep, she said. We will talk tomorrow.

I was grateful to her. My room at the end of the open corridor was large and empty. There was no furniture except for an old desk, a chair, and a bed. In cupboards along the wall I found linens, a lantern, and a pitcher of water. A meal of fish and fruit was laid out on a mat by the bed. I bathed in the sudden silence, by starlight, in a shower with a transparent domed roof. The decorated stone tiles reminded me of my house in Jaffa. Before I fell asleep it crossed my mind that there was no electricity and that I don't like cats, and I didn't understand how I had come to be in this place. Then I slept for ten hours.

The next day was Friday, and I woke to the sounds of the muezzin and the aroma of clove buds. It suddenly hit me that I was in Zanzibar. My head was spinning, and the taste of coconut was on my tongue. I got up. I drank all of the water. From my window I could see the crowd flowing towards the mosques. My hostess sat on a stone bench under a canopy of vines with a leopard-spotted cat on her lap. She looked different. A beehive wig, a robe the color of turmeric, and jewelry inlaid with precious gems made her look like a member of the nobility. She invited me to dine with her and with the orphaned boy whom, so she said, she had adopted as a baby. We sat in the garden and suddenly she said, in Hebrew, I also lived in Jaffa once with my husband who was an Arab businessman. After he died, I came back here. She fell silent, and added with a luminous smile, My whole life I have followed in my family's footsteps . . .

I felt embarrassed. Mr. Caesar had not given me any details, and I did not know how to react. Finally I said that I was glad we had something in common. I added that my room was comfortable and that I had slept well. I had a splitting headache, but I didn't mention it. You are in the Garden of Eden, pronounced Lilliana. At that moment I felt more like in

Hell. We ate pita bread and slices of mango and papaya. The boy brought coffee. You have a headache but it will pass, said Lilliana. You will also get used to talking more. Get a lot of rest. The business is closed until Monday.

And so it happened that in my first three days in Stone Town I did nothing but sleep, eat, and wander around. I didn't know how to be a tourist. I didn't want to be a tourist. The warehouse took up the entire ground floor and stone arches divided the different areas. I asked to start working as soon as possible, and Lilliana gave me a tour of the various sections where the spices were stored by type in sacks, crates, and containers.

She spoke extensively of the way Mr. Caesar's large business was run: she went over the invoices, the orders, and the receipt books that were printed in Swahili, English and German, and stated with satisfaction that they worked in the old-fashioned way that had proven itself over many years. No computers or new technology because of the recurring power failures; it was safer to handwrite. But we did buy a typewriter, she said, and once a year an inspector from the Department of Agriculture makes a visit. A pungent and familiar fragrance overwhelmed me.

I felt better. Lillian called my attention to some urgent orders, dipped a skilled hand into different sacks, touched, smelled, tasted, and seemed to be well-versed in all the elements of the business, which in passing made me wonder why I had been called to come here so urgently.

I asked when the new manager was expected, and Lilliana silently offered me a Cuban cigar which I politely refused. She avidly lit one for herself, swallowed the smoke and said, Soon, Insha'Allah. You've only just arrived.

Her smoking inside the warehouse bothered me, but I did not protest. I also ignored the mouse that crossed my path. The new manager will be responsible for improvements; I am here as a temporary overseer and not a management consultant. I started to work. Whatever I did not understand, Lilliana explained. She was fluent in all the languages and calculations and regarded the spices as her pets. To be honest, I felt really resentful towards her habit of naming the spices, contrary to all the other things that I silently ignored. My attitude towards the spices was thorough and practical, with great respect for expertise, and I would never use childish endearments such as, mama's pampered clove, impertinent peppers, and heavenly cinnamon. To the best of my knowledge, a spice warehouse was a serious and complex business, not a candy store. Once I even tried to write a poem about spices, and it turned out rather dull. Lilliana would observe me and smile.

Is everything okay Moses? Fine, I would say. I didn't know that a face as made-up and furrowed with wrinkles as that of my hostess could be so pleasing to the eye. I said to myself, this is all an illusion.

Two weeks went by and Mr. Caesar called only once. He was very pleased with my report and asked me to be patient because the Indian manager had postponed his arrival. I have to be back in Jaffa by March, I said. I heard a laugh, as if I had told a joke, and then Lilliana's name came up. Was she taking care of me? Had she introduced me to the buyers? Had we traveled? Talked? I said that most of the day I work and that I didn't have too much free time.

I though you would enjoy yourself in Zanzibar, said Mr. Caesar.

I am, I said.

Those two words gave me no rest. Am I enjoying myself? Doing what? When was the last time I enjoyed myself? At night I would try to guess what Lilliana would wear the next day, how she would look, how old she is. The moment I closed my eyes her image would appear before me like a hologram, wrapped in vibrant silk, her bracelets jangling, smoking like a man, speaking in Swahili with the customers. It was torture to be unable to think of anything else. Heavenly cinnamon, heavenly cinnamon, the voice in my head would hum.

After closing up the warehouse we would dine together in the garden or the dining room with the blue-tinted whitewashed walls on the ground floor, talking over the day's events, and as soon as I could I would get up and retire to my room. Again and again I tried to read but the heavenly cinnamon distracted me. There were also power failures, as promised, and the voices of guests coming from Lilliana's quarters. Once she invited me to join them, and I managed to evade the invitation. Another time she sent the boy for me, and I pretended to be asleep. Meanwhile, it had started to rain. From tomorrow, said Lilliana, meals will be served in my apartment. This is our custom every year in the rainy season.

My hostess lived in the southern wing of the house, in a network of high-ceilinged rooms laden with books, carpets, and mementos. To my surprise, there was no dining room table and she encouraged me to wash my hands and sit beside her on a wide velvet-upholstered mattress. Culpa laid before us dishes of mutton, vegetables and fruits, and poured us water with mint leaves. He smiled at me and sat down. Here we return to our roots and eat with our hands, said Lilliana. In her flowing black wig she looked like Cleopatra. Don't be shy, eat, she said and licked her fingers. She wanted to know if I found it tasty, and if there was a dish that I especially liked.

Cinnamon cake, I said. That was a blatant lie. She signaled the boy and he returned with pink coconut cookies.

I thought you might prefer these, she said.

We drank coffee from small porcelain cups. The questions lodged in my throat. Lilliana took out a well-thumbed book entitled *Memoirs of an Arabian Princess from Zanzibar* and said, This is my great grandmother, Salme Said, one of the Sultan's daughters born here in the nineteenth century. She is my ideal. My whole life I have walked in her footsteps.

This confession, spoken in a quiet voice, hit me like a blow to the stomach.

Caesar told me nothing, I said.

I inspected the portrait of the princess on the cover, her determined look, exotic silk attire, her legs crossed, one foot bare and the other foot clad in a wooden-soled sandal, adorned with an abundance of jewelry in the Eastern tradition.

You greatly resemble her, I said to Lilliana.

I want to resemble her in spirit, said my hostess. Salme was intelligent, brave, an adventuress and a great lover of life . . . tragedies only served to strengthen her. I have followed in her footsteps all my life: Germany, Beirut, Jaffa, and Zanzibar. Culpa is a descendant of one of the Sultan's slaves . . . now he is my son. Read the book, and if you go to the museum, you will find many exhibits about my family . . .

I read all night and found it difficult to concentrate the next day. I secretly watched Lilliana. I imagined her in the various stages of her life; say we had met in Jaffa, would that have made me a different person and if so, in what way. What was it in this flamboyant, aging woman that so bewitched and angered me and gave me insomnia?

I waited impatiently for the next meal.

You are a sad man, said Lilliana that evening. You must be taught how to feel happiness. It takes time.

We ate pineapple and sugared almonds. Culpa brought out a flute and began to play.

I will show you the island, said Lilliana. I will take you to the palaces, the plantations, the springs . . . the past is like a garment that fades in the sun; much is destroyed and has disappeared, but the fragrance of cloves remains as it was two hundred years ago, something no conquerors have been able to plunder . . .

And so began our journeys in Zanzibar. Lilliana covered her head with a breathtaking scarf and led me from gate to gate, from mosque to mosque, from palace to palace, up and down the stone alleyways and told me the history of the city and the pink coral-stone houses whose fate was in the hands of strangers who coveted them generation after generation. She slid her hand over the decorative carvings and brass studding of the ancient gates and she urged me to feel the sense of time through the wood. These gates are like people, she said: they have a history of great suffering and pride . . . put your ear against them . . . listen . . . they breathe . . . speak . . . there is an old man in the harbor who understands their language . . . I speak with spices; don't look at me that way, Moses; after you get used to Zanzibar nothing will surprise you anymore . . .

Our daily schedule slowly changed and lost all order and reason. We closed early and went to the market. We wandered among the stalls and everyone greeted Lilliana. In her robes she looked like a brightly-colored flamingo and spoke with passion. Here was the slave market, she said, and here the harem, and that beautiful building over there with the balconies and bell tower is called the House of Wonders, because it was the first house to have electricity and an elevator . . . it belonged to Sultan Barghash . . .

I half-listened to her, because a previous comment of hers occupied my thoughts.

You don't live properly, Lilliana had said. You live on the sidelines . . .

What does it mean to live on the sidelines, I wanted to know. I felt as if my experiences were happening to someone else. We cut open a watermelon and ate it in the shade of the fisherman's hut. We sat on the beach.

My great grandmother Salme ran away with her lover on a boat to Aden and from there to the cold North . . . before she left, she gathered some sand into a pouch as a memento and that sand from Zanzibar is buried with her in Hamburg . . .

Lilliana scooped up some sand, held it to my nose and said, Look Moses, the sand is the same sand. The sea is the same sea. What do you smell? The smell of freedom and love . . .

She entreated me to remove my shoes, and the thought of that caused me discomfort. Even though I had grown up near the Mediterranean, I had never walked barefoot in the sand and never learned to swim. Culpa, who accompanied us everywhere, said, How white your toes are, Mr. Moses, and Lilliana laughed and gathered sea shells into her sandals.

You feel good now, right?

I feel good, I said.

On the weekends we drove out to the spice plantations in the center of the island. As a spice merchant I knew a great deal about the origin and cultivation of my merchandise, but just as I would imagine coffee importers never wandered to remote coffee farms and were satisfied with knowing the types of beans and their taste, so had I never visited a spice plantation. Lilliana was greeted with hugs and kisses and introduced me to all the laborers. She bounded from shrub to shrub and from tree to tree like a young girl, touching and smelling and licking and chewing the nutmeg, the cardamom, the vanilla, and the cinnamon, and encouraged me to join her. The plantation was buzzing with bees, and after the rain an enormous rainbow stretched across the sky.

We are in the Garden of Eden, said Lilliana.

And the bees are angels, added Culpa.

My tongue, eyes, and the palms of my hands were on fire. I felt pinpricks all over. I did not cry when my parents and my wife died. I could not cry in the presence of others and even less in my own company. On my first visit to the plantations I shed a tear.

I'm allergic, I said.

You are happy, said Lilliana. Tomorrow we will go to Bububu, where once, on her plantation by the sea, my great grandmother Salme was also very happy.

We went to Bububu. We helped the women of the village gather seaweed, crabs, and octopus during low tide. We exchanged greetings with the boat builders on the beach. A gust of wind from the direction of Pemba carried in a fresh wave of clove fragrance. We sat on the white sand under the coconut palms and ate bananas and passion fruit that we had bought on the way.

Tell me about your wife, asked Lilliana.

She was a good woman, I said.

What else . . .

She always had the same hairdo . . .

I touched the Hamsa on my neck. My whole body ached.

My hair fell out long ago, said Lilliana; that is why I wear wigs all the time. I once got lost in the Sahara desert and Berbers attacked me and held me hostage. I told them about my great grandmother Salme's childhood in the Sultan's harem in Zanzibar, and they were bewitched; they gave me a horse and released me. I discovered that my hair had turned white during my captivity. I married young with white hair. In Jaffa they called me "fairy."

Lilliana gazed hesitantly at the pendant.

Your wife once sewed me a wonderful dress, she said suddenly. I came for fittings in the evenings, and once you walked into the room and said, Excuse me, with an embarrassed smile. Your wife was wearing that pendant . . . she said that you were the most devoted husband in the world.

I cried until daybreak. Later I quietly went down to my office in the warehouse and lit a cigar. I fed the cats. Heavenly cinnamon, I said out loud.

Months passed. I extended the rental agreement for my business in Jaffa, and I ceased asking about the new manager. The parrots learned how to say my name. Moses, Lilli, they screech all day. I read a lot about Zanzibar. Tend the garden. Learn Swahili. Play chess with Culpa. Sometimes we stay at the plantations for several days, drink coffee with the laborers, tease one another and laugh. My heart is filled with anticipation for the coming day. Lilliana calmly combs her wigs, makes her eyes up with mascara till they look like enormous starfish, and constantly changes her appearance. In her colorful Khanga robes and jewelry inlaid with precious gems, she looks like an ancient queen. Caesar calls now and then, promises to visit sometime and find out what happened to the Indian manager. He always praises my work, asks about Lilliana and says, I knew she would wait for you.

I keep silent. That sentence remains a puzzle.

We will go to Jaffa together some day, says Lilliana.

Jaffa or Zanzibar, does it matter? A new city was born in my heart.

~

When dealing with people,
remember you are not dealing with creatures of logic,
but creatures of emotion. — Dale Carnegie

The All-Knowing Eye

Andrea Vojtko

Garland Duckett grabbed his navy blazer and told the secretary at McPherson's Realty he was going to lunch. He thought it best not to tell her he was really heading over to Huntley Meadows to talk with God. Huntley Meadows was a nature center near his workplace in Alexandria, Virginia, so he could make it over there in fifteen minutes, even if he stopped at the Krispy Kreme first to get a couple of raspberry-filled doughnuts and some coffee, which he planned to gobble down on his way to the park. Then he would hurry out to the boardwalk that was built over the marsh until God made his appearance. He was convinced that God resided in the body of a Great Blue Heron that he saw there regularly.

Garland's first visit to Huntley Meadows was six months earlier when a client raved about its being so near the house he was trying to sell. His client bought the property, and he made a nice profit. Afterwards they stopped by the park and he felt exhilarated as his client pointed out birds in the marsh pond.

When he came home with the good news about the sale, his wife, Kelly, announced that she and Matt, his closest friend at McPherson's, were having an affair and were planning to move to Phoenix. His world changed in an instant, and his euphoria turned to grief. He ran from the house and drove around aimlessly until he found himself back at Huntley Meadows where he had felt such elation earlier. And then

God in the guise of a Great Blue Heron made his first appearance.

When Garland finished his last doughnut and turned into the nearly vacant parking lot at Huntley Meadows, the sun had begun its descent. It was 3 p.m. on a Friday afternoon in late spring. He strode down the trail until he got to the boardwalk and continued walking to the spot where it split into two branches. Taking the less-used one, he wandered over to an expansive observation area and stopped. Resting his arms on a wooden rail, he gazed below at a large turtle in the marsh. Tall reeds surrounded the swamp which was secluded and quiet at that hour.

As he looked up, the Great Blue Heron appeared – not six feet from him. It looked like a small, four-foot dinosaur or some type of prehistoric creature with large commanding golden eyes that seemed to be all-knowing the way they gazed directly at him, as though they had some deep understanding of his inner thoughts. Garland looked straight into the heron's golden eyes.

"Good, you're here again," he said to the heron whose black saber-like bill was pointed straight ahead. He sighed. "Feelin' kind of low. You know, about Kelly and Matt. I should have challenged him to a duel," he joked. Garland was an expert fencer having learned the skill when he played Hamlet in the Alexandria Little Playhouse. "I lunged at him in the office, but two secretaries held me back. He just sneered at me."

The heron's violet-blue feathers were shimmering, accented with a light plum color around his long neck. He seemed to give Garland his full attention.

"The guy's rich but he's a thief. I told her that. Kelly said,

'You can't live in a fantasy world forever, Garland.'" He shook his head back and forth. Garland knew he was a little strange but Kelly used to call him unique, like it was a good thing.

The heron looked at him earnestly and seemed to be sympathetic.

"Kelly changed last year. She didn't want to do the things we always did together. Didn't want to fly kites in Potomac Park, didn't want to go to the theater, and didn't want to visit the cherry blossoms in the spring." Garland wiped his eyes with his sleeve. "We were married for ten years."

The heron raised his left foot as though he were about to take another step but stood there with his foot riveted in mid-air. Garland thought he should sum up.

"So here I am thirty-five. My wife and friend gone off to Phoenix, and I'm making almost daily visits to this marsh to see you. I could use a sign, if you are God, to guide me." Garland reflected that stranger things happen in Shakespeare's plays. He looked at the heron and gasped, "I need your help. I'm desperate," and then stumbled back to his car.

~

On Saturday morning Garland woke at 6 a.m., turned over, and went back to bed dreaming about someone banging on his front door. He heard sounds from a dump truck below his window and some loud male voices as he lapsed in and out of sleep. A breeze wafted into his open window, bringing with it the smell of late spring gardening, finally waking him at 10 a.m. The smell was pungent. Someone must be mulching in the gardens, he thought.

The wind picked up and the odor became even stronger. When he opened his eyes he saw dirt blowing through his window. Jumping out of bed in alarm, he looked outside.

"Ah!" He put his hand on his heart. There was a pile of mulch on the 15x15 foot plot in front of his townhouse high enough to touch with the foil he kept under his bed. He reached for it, sensing trouble afoot. His view of the street was partially blocked by the mulch, but he could see two kids on the sidewalk in front of his neighbor's house staring up at the enormous pile. There was a murmuring below, and he suspected others were out there hidden from his view. He put the foil down and ran around the bedroom trying to find some pants to throw over his shorts, and a tee shirt. Cramming his feet into his Nikes and leaving the laces flapping against the floor, he took the foil with him and bounded down the stairs. As he opened the front door, a piece of paper fell at his feet. The delivery form was for the next street over, 17th Street instead of 17th Road, where he lived, and the addressee was a Chelsea Rosebery.

The mulch pile spread from the wall of his house, obliterating his garden, to the sidewalk and even as far as the tree lawn that bordered the street. Astounding in scale, it completely covered the stone path to his porch, as well as the seven porch steps, preventing him from exiting his house without walking through hip-high mulch. He looked at it with wonder.

"What exactly are you planning to do with this mulch?" Marlene Higgins, his next door neighbor, screamed at him over the hill of dirt, her elfin features distorted into a scowl.

"It's a mistake. I didn't order it," he gestured with his foil, which he then set aside after Marlene rolled her eyes. He was reminded of Matt's sneer after he lunged at him.

"I'll say it's a mistake," she shouted. Several other

townhouse residents joined her and the two kids in front of her house, mouthing words of discouragement over the mountain of mulch.

He hollered over to his neighbors thirty feet away, waving the delivery paper. "It was sent to the wrong address. It should have been delivered to a Chelsea Rosebery on Seventeenth Street."

"How are you going to get it over there?" Marlene demanded.

"I don't know," Garland stammered. "I'll call the delivery guy." He fumbled with the delivery papers and bumped his head into the storm door. "I'll call them," he promised, waving the papers at Marlene and other neighbors who had joined her to denounce the eyesore on his lawn.

"Ma'am, but I didn't order any mulch."

"Why didn't you tell that to the delivery man?"

"I was asleep."

"You should have been awake to receive the mulch."

"I didn't order the mulch," he said.

"Well, then what is the problem?"

"There's been a mistake. Your deliveryman dumped the mulch at the wrong address. He dumped it at Forty-Five Ten Seventeenth Road and he should have dumped it at Forty-Five Ten Seventeenth Street."

"Let me see, Sir. I have a copy of the shipping address here. It says Forty-Five Ten Seventeenth Street. Isn't that your address?"

"No. There's a difference between Street and Road. They're different addresses."

"Just a minute, Sir. I have to check with my supervisor." The phone went on hold. Now there was banging on the

117

backdoor of Garland's townhouse which continued while he grasped the phone tightly for ten minutes before he heard a click and then the recorded message, "If you would like to make a call, please hang up and dial again . . ."

Garland hung up the phone and put his head in his hands. The hammering on his backdoor continued. He got up slowly to answer the door.

"What? What is it?" he said opening the back door. A warrior-like woman stood there, her heavyset body twice as large as Garland's, who was a trim six feet.

"Garland Duckett?"

"Yes."

"I'm Pearl Burgher, Chair of the Condo Covenants Committee for the Fox Ridge townhouses."

He heard of her and knew she wasn't someone to cross.

"You are in extreme violation of Section Thirty-Four of the Condo covenants document for the Fox Ridge townhouses," she continued.

"But I was sleeping. How could I commit a violation when I was sleeping?" He felt overwhelmed and wished Kelly were around to deal with this absurd situation. He had enough trouble coping with the ordinary.

"That is a disgrace out there. It's an eyesore and a health hazard. You have twenty-four hours to get rid of that obscene pile of mulch on your front lawn."

"How am I going to get someone here on the weekend?"

"You should have thought about that when you took delivery."

"I was asleep when it was delivered."

"What kind of person can sleep through a ton of manure being dumped on him?"

Garland thought about that while Pearl searched through her tote bag vigorously. The image of Kelly and Matt on a golf course in Arizona floated into his head.

"Get rid of the mulch or you'll be charged fifty dollars each day that it stays there," Pearl said and slapped him with a Condo Covenants Committee summons. Garland closed the door, his pulse racing. Sitting down in his kitchen for a few minutes, he did some deep breathing exercises from the Yoga classes Kelly insisted he take early in their marriage. He could not bear to call the shipping company again but was in a quandary about what he should do.

Chelsea Rosebery. That was the answer. She ordered this mulch. He looked through his blinds and could not see anyone else waiting to jump on him, so he grabbed his nylon windbreaker and went out to find her house.

~

He rang the bell on the front portico of 4510 17th Street. What a mansion, he thought. He remembered when it was up for sale eight years ago with seven bedrooms, four baths, a swimming pool, Jacuzzi, finished basement, finished attic. The door opened slowly and a tall, willowy woman was visible behind the screen door.

"Chelsea Rosebery?"

"Yes?"

"Hello, I'm Garland Duckett," he said.

"What a lovely name – Garland," she said in a hushed tone.

"I have your mulch," he said.

"Oh, just pull up around the back and pile it next to the greenhouse." She opened the door and came outside.

"No. I mean. Your mulch is on my front lawn. I live on Seventeenth Road and the deliveryman made a mistake and dumped the mulch on my front lawn." Garland emboldened his tenor voice.

"Oh." She paused, putting her long thin fingers on her cheek. Garland noticed how clear and flawless her skin was and how symmetrical her features appeared. She would be a good Rosalind in *As You Like It.* "What should we do?"

"I think we have quite a dilemma here. It's a lot of mulch."

"Oh, but I need that much. I'm making a wildlife nature preserve in my backyard. Would you like to see it?"

Chelsea's voice mesmerized Garland. It was soft and light and faded in and out like a whisper. He thought of Kelly's more assertive voice and then answered, "Yes. Yes, I would." Chelsea led him around back. She was as tall as he was and moved gracefully as she walked around in a gossamer full-length lavender gown imprinted with small gold butterflies.

"What beautiful landscaping," he said to her as they walked into her backyard.

"Yes, but I want it to be more natural. I want to create a marsh to attract birds and wildlife," she said in a breathless hush. "There are five acres here."

"That sounds very nice. I often visit the marshlands at Huntley Meadows to see the birds there," he said.

"I love Huntley Meadows," she answered. She could have been a sorceress the way her hazel eyes, with their golden specs and her faint smile, held his gaze. Kelly had agitating eyes that darted around her surroundings like fireflies.

"I'm building a backyard habitat. I have the perfect land for it," Chelsea said, looking across the forested land and meadows behind her house. "Soon the wildflowers will be in bloom." Twenty-five bird feeders and birdhouses were spread throughout her property. "All I have to do is add a marshy area and I'm sure I can attract many rare creatures here."

"You can make your own little Huntley Meadows in your backyard," he encouraged her.

"Yes, I have something like that in mind. And let me show you my sunroom." She led him up the steps in the back onto an expansive deck.

Garland was enthralled when he saw the marbleized deep-green Jacuzzi hot tub in the corner of the deck. He went over to it and ran his fingers over the smooth ceramic interior.

"It helps my aching body in the morning," Chelsea said. He smiled and couldn't help picturing her naked for a brief moment. She was quite a lovely, ephemeral woman. She led him through French doors to a sunroom like none he had ever seen in all of his years as a realtor. It was as large as his whole downstairs with arched, designer windows everywhere, and several birding scopes set up around the room directed toward the backyard.

"This is amazing. Just amazing," he said.

"But we're forgetting about the mulch problem," Chelsea reminded him.

"Problems are made to be solved," he said with a cavalier wave of his hand. "It's just mulch. We'll get it over here some way."

"Would you like some wine and cheese?" she said; "It's getting close to lunchtime."

"That sounds wonderful," he answered. "I think I deserve a little relief after the traumas of the morning."

"I'm so sorry this happened to you," she said.

Garland joked, "The Condo Covenants Committee at Fox Ridge is on my case for this. You'd think it was World War Three."

"But I don't want to cause you any trouble."

"No," he said, accepting his wine in a beautifully etched crystal goblet. "All we need to do is find someone with a dump truck."

"My landscaper has a dump truck."

"Really? So there you go."

"I'll just call my landscaper to pick it up and bring it over here."

"That would be the fastest way to solve the problem," Garland said, pleased that Chelsea had provided the means to resolve the issue so effortlessly. He began to relax on the couch while enjoying his wine and cheese. Over the next half-hour they talked about the marshlands and consumed the entire bottle of wine. Chelsea opened another bottle of White Zinfandel with its rose blush and poured some in his glass.

"Delightful," he said feeling quite drunk.

"I plan to build a wetland stretching from the river birch to the sycamore," she continued; "I hope to attract not only birds but turtles, foxes, beavers . . ."

Yes, and maybe rats, mice and other vermin, Garland, the realtor, thought. But he said, "How fascinating, a wildlife habitat right here." If his Fox Ridge neighbors realized what Chelsea was planning in their backyard, the mulch pile in front of his house would not be their biggest concern.

"And do you live here alone?" he asked.

"Yes, except when my daughter visits. She goes to Berkeley, my alma mater. My ex-husband is long gone. But he left me with a nice settlement." She waved her arm around the place. "He wasn't about to spend his life with an aging poet."

"Oh, you're a poet. Remember what Antony said about Cleopatra, 'Age cannot wither her, nor custom stale her infinite variety,'" Garland said.

"You are so generous with your Shakespearean perceptions," Chelsea said smiling, her eyebrows raised in surprise at his dramatic prowess.

Women were always so concerned about their age, Garland thought. She looked just fine to him, maybe five years older than he was. He was now deeply drunk, and Kelly and Matt receded far into the background of his mind. Chelsea moved elegantly around the room in her lavender gown. How appropriate, he thought, that she's a poet.

"Your dress is the same color as the White Zinfandel," he said.

"What a wonderful metaphor," she said glancing at her dress and then the wine.

She sat next to him, glass in hand, and began reciting one of her poems. He heard words like "tangerine," "dancing," "blossom," "wreath," "mingling," "lyre," "altar" but he had lost the ability to tie them together in any meaningful way.

"Beautiful, beautiful," he said.

"It's so rare to find a man who can listen so intently to poetry," she said, moving close to him to whisper the last line. "Because the chalice is full and Athene beckons."

He felt his pulse beating now as he realized she had nothing on under her multilayer diaphanous dress. Leaning toward him, her breasts were visible. He had all he could do to keep from throwing his head into her cleavage and was trying hard to think about the mulch, the heron, his ex-wife, and his former friend. But he could see only the curves of her breasts, her waist and abdomen as she continued to recite an avalanche of verses that made no sense to him except for occasional images that the words evoked, "liquid gold," "pomegranate," "pale blue sky." He was trying hard to recover himself when she said. "Not so bad for a fiftyish poet, is it?"

My God, she is nearly twenty years older than me, he thought. What would Matt and Kelly think of him? Here he was nearly swirling into her breasts. Think about the mulch. Visualize. Visualize a pile of mulch in front of your house. But he was in a state of intoxication and dreaminess that was entrenched and only promised to get worse as Chelsea reached over to pour some more wine into his glass. Abruptly, he put the glass down.

"I must go," he said, "the mulch."

"Oh, yes, the mulch," she said.

"The mulch," they both said in unison.

Garland got up, staggering, bumping into scopes and floor cushions. He groped his way to the deck, looking back at the poet following like Athene behind him, her lavender gown blowing in the breeze. The fresh air helped to revive him slightly, but he stumbled across Chelsea's lawn waving back to her, occasionally murmuring "Mulch," and she in return called after him, "The mulch, yes."

~

Garland got up at 5 a.m. on Sunday to the smell of the mulch that now permeated his townhouse. He decided to go into work instead of facing the scrutiny of Pearl Burgher who started her incessant walks with her dog at 6 a.m. Before he went, he shoveled some of the mulch into a trash bag and put it into the trunk of his car.

After spending an hour on a few pending contracts at McPherson's Realty, Garland left the office and drove over to Huntley Meadows. The parking lot at the marshland was full as the sun ascended. He walked briskly on the trail leading to the boardwalk and then stopped at the spot where the sacred heron often came. After twenty minutes of waiting, the heron appeared several feet away and stood silently staring at him in the morning sunlight, looking so beautiful with the lavender hue around his neck.

"I had quite an adventure yesterday," he said to the heron; "But I managed to get through it, managed to deal with a lot of unsavory characters. And then I got out of a pretty sticky situation with an attractive older woman. I've been in enough Shakespearean comedies to recognize a comic situation when I saw it."

"Oh, look, Mommy," a little girl said coming over to the heron. Garland wasn't prepared for this infringement on his personal space with God. He looked at the child and then decided to ignore these people who, he reasoned, he would never see again, and continued talking to the heron.

"The mulch was a perfect sign. I felt a lot better yesterday visiting with Chelsea. I brought some mulch as an offering," he said to the heron.

The little girl's mother had now joined her and glared at Garland as he conversed with the heron. Garland opened the bag of mulch with the heron still staring at him, his foot lifted, transfixed in space. He spilled the mulch into the marsh in front of the heron, and the bird immediately spread out his wings and flew away, grazing Garland's head.

"Ah!" the little girl screamed.

"What's wrong with you?" her mother yelled at Garland.

Garland stood riveted to the spot for the moment. He walked away slowly, wondering why God left like that. He consoled himself by thinking that maybe God planned to appear at some other place to lead him on the right path.

~

The next morning Chelsea's landscape company came early and began shoveling the mulch into a dump truck with a back hoe. When he saw from his window they were making good progress, he went out to observe with the rest of the neighborhood. After they got the mulch loaded and had hosed down his yard and sidewalks, there was no sign that the mulch had ever been there. He considered walking to Chelsea's to thank her for getting the job done so efficiently, but the image of her bare breasts floated into his head and he decided it was better to forget the whole episode, lest he lose his self-control. He could imagine Kelly and Matt's sarcasm if they ever knew he was with a woman old enough to be his mother.

Garland went to Huntley Meadows several times the next week but the sacred heron was not there. He clung to the hope that God would appear somewhere else to lead him down the right path. By Friday, he decided not to go back to Huntley Meadows; it seemed pointless to visit without God there.

~

Two weeks later he sat on his deck drinking some White Zinfandel to lift his spirits. The heron had not appeared to him and he was depressed. The wine made him feel drowsy and relaxed. Chelsea's favorite wine, he thought, taking another sip. Half-asleep, he moved in and out of his dreams, aware that he was on the deck, but seeing images of Kelly with Matt, kites blowing in the air, the Great Blue Heron, he and Matt bicycling over a rugged trail, Chelsea gliding across her deck in her lavender gown, the plum-colored feathers on the heron's neck and Chelsea again.

He woke suddenly, the latter images still with him. He felt an intense desire to hear Chelsea recite her poetry. He poured some more wine and thought, "Her voice was ever soft, gentle and low, an excellent thing in women." Chelsea was so whimsical and Kelly and Matt were "manured with industry." Lines from the plays he had memorized were rising to the top of his consciousness. Chelsea was a "very" Chelsea and he was a "very" Garland, like Antony and Cleopatra. Sipping his wine, he felt proud of his own ability to pull words and thoughts at will from Shakespearean plays. Images of Chelsea's graceful hands, sensuous lips, flowing robes, rounded breasts floated in and out. Why should he care about her age? She was a rare woman, the kind one usually meets only on stage.

He needed to take action or else he would become like Hamlet. Getting up from his lounge chair a little tipsy, he sleepwalked over to 17th Street carrying with him a full bottle of White Zinfandel. It had been three weeks since the mulch delivery and he should inquire about the backyard habitat.

Chelsea opened the door and greeted him on the portico, dressed alluringly in a long white silk gown.

"You look like the Empress Josephine," he said. She smiled and seemed pleased to see him.

"It's my tribute to Christina Rossetti," she said. "Did you notice the garlands in my hair?"

He blushed at the play on his name as she turned her head to reveal some fresh violets woven through her elegantly-styled hair.

"Very nice," he said circling behind her to examine her intricate hair arrangement, his heart pounding against his chest.

"You move so gracefully, like a dancer," she said.

"I'm a fencer," Garland said, assuming the "on guard" position with the wine bottle acting as the sword.

"Fencing, how gallant. It suits you," she said half-whispering. Garland glowed at the praise.

"I've come over to see the wildlife habitat," Garland said.

"It's wonderful," she said, clasping her hands together over her bosom.

Garland entered the house through the front door. The living room had carved molding on the ceilings, Grecian vases, colorful silk pillows, large medieval tapestries, the fragrance of fresh fruit in golden bowls, and the sound of haunting flute music in the background. Garland turned slowly in a circle to take everything in. Matt or Kelly would never appreciate the sensuousness of this room, he thought.

Chelsea led him into the sunroom with its many scopes now looking out to the new marsh that had completely transformed the backyard.

"Just like Huntley Meadows," he said with pleasure.

"Come out," she said. He put the bottle on the coffee table and went with Chelsea out to the deck and then into the backyard. They walked over the freshly cut grass toward the meadow which was blooming with spring wild flowers. Chelsea picked some and twirled toward Garland. He smiled at her, beginning to feel the hypnotic sense he did the last time he was with her. He went over to the new marsh which had a small boardwalk built over it. Chelsea walked up to it like a Greek goddess.

"Fantastic," he said shaking his head in astonishment.

"And you should see the wildlife it attracts," she said; "This morning I saw two solitary sandpipers on this very spot." She looked at him with a subtle smile which he shyly returned.

"I would love to hear some of your poems," he implored.

Chelsea began reciting one of her poems, her soft voice so soothing, so comforting to Garland. He looked into her eyes and a vivid image of the heron floated into his mind. When she finished, he said, "I often see a Great Blue Heron at Huntley Meadows who has these all-knowing eyes."

"All-knowing eyes – how wonderful!" she whispered so near his ear he could feel her breath.

~

The merit of human actions springs from their motive;
and disinterestedness is their crowning virtue. – La Bruyère

White Kaleidoscope

Kelly Wantuch

As I lie on the cool cement garden bench next to the Japanese maple, I close my eyes and try to imagine that the streaming sweep of the incoming airplanes is a pulsating drift of lake waves gently hitting my canoe. Then I am abruptly reminded, on this glorious Saturday morning, of the fighting couple next door who announce, through their open window, who is cheating on whom. The neighbor across the alley is fixing his Studebaker Lark convertible, loudly revving the engine, as if he can resurrect his good old days. The cobbled-stoned waterfall and pond I built helps detach me from the noise of Portage Ave., but it was a failed experiment. The day-glo-orange koi, almost on cue, dash to the surface looking for a possible treat, all trained to be taken out of my hand. At forty years old, I feel like those koi, pacing around in a rubber-lined pond inhaling chemically-treated water, trained to want someone else's idea of a good life.

There is an unspoken neighborhood competition every summer about who can have the most perfect-looking lawn. My neighbors leave for work in their BMW's with cell phones ironed to their ears, always too busy to notice a wave or hello. They don't even stop and admire their professionally planted Victoria Blue salvia and French marigolds growing in perfect geometric designs along their razor-edged driveways. The neighbor's poodle is yapping again because of another falsely triggered car alarm. There is no croaking of frogs to be heard at dusk, there are no night crawlers popping into their holes in the glare of a shining flashlight, and now I have asthma, semi-controlled by steroids. It is as if I am on twenty-four-hour surveillance, with neighbors able to peer into my backyard from their second story windows at any time. I don't need much, and expensive, mass-produced consumer goods don't really matter to me; I don't need a McDonald's close by. But I guess I have always been different.

If I close my eyes and try hard enough, I remember how good things used to feel, and I can remember a summer when my father's stained, metallic-smelling hands slowly turned white and soft. It was the year he said we would go fishing every day after he quit his factory job, the year he took off the entire summer before opening a soon-to-be-busy TV repair business. I was only ten years old.

~

The sun reluctantly wanted to rise around 5:30 a.m. that morning. Sitting at the kitchen table, I restlessly waited for my father finally to get up. I was replacing the dirty blue fishing line that had been snapped by an unexpected pike late last summer. I wasn't a girlie girl: I knew how to fish, I knew how to string a line, and yes, I wormed my own hook.

My father was usually up the earliest, drinking coffee, scarfing down his breakfast in three big gulps, and rushing out the door on his way to a job he called "the race to death." Today was different; it was the first day he didn't have to go to that noisy, mechanical, impersonal place. This time I was up before him, all dressed and breakfast made just as he taught me: black coffee, fried eggs with ketchup, thick sliced bacon, and toast. I had already packed two lunches: two slices of old fashioned loaf on whole wheat bread with brown mustard and a tiny bit of horseradish, my father's favorite sandwich. He'd always said I made the best sandwiches.

My heart was beating fast because today we were going to find East Lake, a hidden lake across the dirt road from our house, the one we discovered on an old county map at the Elkhart County Historical Museum. We had lived in our secluded country house for a couple of years and had no idea there was a small public lake located within a half mile in the middle of our neighboring Amish farmlands. There was no public access, and it couldn't be seen from the road because of all the hills, hills large enough to host every year the Iron Horseman Hill Climb Championships.

~

I knew these Amish pastures well. I loved to play in the gullies for hours, looking for the perfect hideout and finding old thrown-away junk. I frequented one certain gully in the back-woods that was used as a junkyard, until the neighbors started discarding their cut up cow parts. Maybe it was due to a disease or maybe the cows became crippled. Eventually, I found the perfect place, a deep and narrow gully that was covered thick in briars all the way around but open on the inside. I made an entry just big enough that I could crawl through without it being noticed from the outside. It concealed me and all my stuff, even in the winter when the leaves had fallen away from the bushes.

I found an old baby highchair that had one leg missing, so I hack-sawed off the others and leveled it just right in the dirt so it would recline. This was my best prize find, and since I was a skinny kid, it fit my body perfectly. While leaning back, I could look up to the sky through all the branches overhead, and if I blurred my eyes enough it reminded me of looking through a kaleidoscope of white, brown, and blue designs. I dug a narrow dirt shelf on one side of the gully next to my chair where I displayed my collection of found treasures: old brown and blue medicine bottles, horseshoes, various spice cans and other neat looking things whose original use was unknown. I also found a chipped, rusty porcelain bowl which stored my ever-revolving stash of old 1960's National Geographic magazines. When I became hungry there was always something to eat without going home: wild black raspberries, strawberries, mulberries, little sour apples off the trees, sweet white and lavender clover flowers, and crisp young kernelless field corn.

In the summer, my narrow hideout felt cool and damp against my skin, like the stone walls of an old cellar during the hottest days. I brought a small canvas tarp from home that I tied to the overhead branches all rolled up and ready to use as a rain shield. I loved the hollow tapping on the canvas when it rained, like someone playing a hand drum, and many times the soft sound lulled me to sleep for hours. In autumn, I had to peel off penny sized reddish-brown ticks that seemed to have become magnetized to my scalp. I sliced them into equal parts with an old steak knife, and it amazed me how much blood they could hold in their bellies. In the winter I made little fires to keep my hands and feet warm. I even tried, with a girlfriend once, to smoke dried, hollow weeds that were sticking out of the snow, until the inhaled black smoke burnt our throats raw – we vowed never to smoke again. I loved my special place; I could read all day, watch the birds, animals and bugs around me, and daydream for hours without being bothered by anyone.

~

With fishing poles in hand, our lunches in brown paper sacks, and crescent shaped leather canteens filled with cold well water hanging around our necks, we both walked fast, as if we were beagles on a hot trail of rabbit tracks. The ankle-high dewy grass made my blue Converse sneakers wet all the way through to my toes and gave me a chill. I am not sure if the chill was from the crispness of the dew or the excitement I felt going on an adventure with my father. I climbed through many barbed-wired fences along the way, strands my father held apart with his worn leather work boots. Trampling through the deep layers of fallen leaves and sticks of squirrel infested woods, we didn't care if we made too much noise since we weren't rabbit hunting.

The grass was now dry, it seemed as if we had been walking in circles for many hours, and I was getting tired. As we walked out of the woods and down a hill, the ground started to feel springy to the step and the air felt heavy. We soon came upon a wide ditch, and we had no choice other than to go through it. Dad said he would go first, and as he stepped closer to the edge of the water, he suddenly plummeted deeply into the wet black muck all the way to his waist. I wasn't sure if I should laugh or feel terrified because he couldn't move his legs; he was really stuck. He handed me his fishing pole and told me to pull him out. I stood there, not certain what I should do; I was scared, and I didn't want to fall in, but I knew better than to disobey him. With all my weight I dragged him out slowly; he was covered in black and smelled like the neighboring hog farm. The excitement of the day soon left his eyes as he said we had better get back home. I was feeling disappointed, too, but I knew he wouldn't give up. He would find a way to that lake. Our journey would continue.

~

Shortly after our failed attempt, my father found out that for three dollars, Orva, the Amish neighbor, would allow us access through his field paths leading to the lake. Finding this out was rather difficult since the Amish tend to be very quiet about secret trails; perhaps this is because they respect the land and don't want anyone, especially "the English," to mess it up. But since we always let them use our telephone, they divulged their secret. Orva even gave us brown chicken eggs when we would return from our fishing trips; he knew how to be neighborly after all. We eventually bought our milk from him — thick, unpasteurized cow's milk that would stick deliciously to the sides of a drinking glass.

The small kidney-shaped lake was located at the bottom of three pasture hills, hills where cows and work horses grazed on grass next to the fenced-off corn fields. At the bottom of the hill was an overturned green canoe stored under a solitary white oak tree. The lake's perimeter was almost completely overgrown with cattails. The only way into the lake was by a narrow path through which only a slender canoe could maneuver. Along the path we could sometimes see jelly black-peppered frog eggs, after the surprise of their parents diving for cover. Male red-winged black birds foraging in the cattails gave their warning barks as I came near their sparrow-looking mates hiding in mud-packed homemade baskets of grass and moss. This lake reminded me of one of my favorite novels as a child, *The Secret Garden*. Contained within the thick walls of cattails was a nature sanctuary, as within the walls of the garden in that story. There were no houses, motor boats, and no people, except maybe a straw-hatted farmer singing in Pennsylvania Dutch as he worked in his fields.

The water was so clear we could see the fish nibbling the bait from many feet away, their multi-colored bodies floating just above the lake's sandy bottom. Dragon flies would hover above the placid water, fighting each other over who would get to land on the bobber, sometimes sharing. Then when I got a nibble, the dragon flies would flee, frightened, as the bobber dipped into the rippling water.

There was a feeling of peace watching my dad finally able to relax – he leaned back against his boat seat with a long exhalation. We didn't need to talk; we just enjoyed being with each other in such natural serenity. Even though I was fiercely afraid of the water (because of a near-drowning incident when I was three) somehow I felt protected here. Feeling the coolness of the metal canoe against my bare feet, I could close my eyes and almost fall asleep in the hot sun, keeping my fingers in contact of the line in case I would get a bite. My wormy, fish-smelling hands didn't even bother me while eating my lunch. As my father promised, we spent many days that summer fishing almost every day. But there is a time during that summer I remember best, a time almost magical.

One evening we were heading back home just before dusk, after a mostly unsuccessful attempt at catching fish. We had only caught a few small crappie and lake perch, stored in our wire basket hanging over the side of the canoe. I liked to drag my line through the water at the back of the canoe as my father paddled, hoping to attract an enormous bass. And that was what I was doing when all of a sudden, a heavy hit pulled the line tight with tension and swirled the back of the canoe around. Dad got all excited and grabbed my pole before the fish took me and the pole into the weeds. Excited about finally catching a large bass, he pulled it in and I scooped it up with the net. It was an eight inch bluegill. Feeling rather inspired, we kept fishing and energetically caught one fish after another. Then the lightening bugs came out, little flashing lighthouses warning us to come back to shore because it was getting dark. The night was cloudy, and so in the country it was as dark as a cave, like coal. We had to pull the hooks out by feel, carefully. There were no lights to guide us back through the little path out of the lake. We finally found our way out, by luck really; dad said we would have to stay out all night if we couldn't find our way. Maybe he was just kidding. I am not sure I would have minded, since the experience was dream-like, pleasant and reassuring.

When we got back home and looked under the porch light we counted that we had caught eighteen bluegills. Because they were so big, dad filleted the thick meat, which was better than picking out the sharp bones. Even though it was late and everyone else had gone to bed, we were hungry, so we dipped the fillets into some homemade beer batter and fried those fish for a late night supper.

~

Maybe it's the nostalgia of the memory, but I swear no fish has ever tasted as good as it did that night. Maybe that is why I love sushi; I miss that fresh fish taste, or maybe it is something else, an intangible feeling. Tonight when I remembered East Lake I decided to find it on a satellite map and discovered where the lake was located in relation to the old house. I was happy to see the large oak tree with the canoe still under it by the edge of the lake. But as I scanned the on-screen map to view the entire lake area, I felt heaviness within my gut. There were now three sprawling, enormous, million dollar mansions, with glowing green golf-course-like lawns.

To my mortification, I saw that each massive structure had a winding private drive leading to the lake.

Feeling numb and wanting to hide away from the world, I clicked off the map page, shut down my computer, watched the white screen fragment into darkness, and felt keenly a natural instinct of wanting to crawl into a hidden gully.

~

Don't let us forget that the causes of human actions are
usually immeasurably more complex and varied than our
subsequent explanations of them. — Dostoyevsky

Through the Wagonwheel

Larry Eby

The man held the hose between his denim-covered knees, put his hands in the path of the flickering water and scrubbed the blood and soil from his cracked palms and fingernails. Cloudy water pooled around his ropers and he shifted, sinking slightly into the mud. He nodded to the woman near a grouping of Joshua trees and she twisted the spigot until the water ceased.

The man beckoned her to follow and they walked in silence to the barn. Increasing winds drove sand into their eyes. The woman pulled the hood of her parka over tangled ebony hair as the man struggled with the barn door. The red paint of the wooden door was faded and chipping away. She helped slide it open and they entered.

A Ford Ranger pulled up in the driveway around noon.
Who's that? she said, sliding her fingers off the piano keys.
He looked out the window. You expecting anyone?
Not today.
An overweight man struggled out of the truck with an envelope clutched between his fingers.

He closed the sliding door and peered around the shelter. A few penciled lines on the wall, marking the height of his father's fathers, and his mark was an inch lower than the rest. There were three bales of hay stacked on the far end with a hook lying on the top and another lodged into the side of a bale. The inside was dim, clouded with dust that drifted from the bare ground below their soles as they shuffled to the first stall of three. It reeked of blood and excrement. The stall door, the bottom half a solid square of steel and the top half steel bars like a jail cell painted maroon, was open and he stepped over the framing into the stall. The woman held onto the edges of her parka hood, keeping her eyes away from the center of the stall. He motioned for her to come in.

The doorbell rang. He answered the door. The messenger was sweaty.
What can I help you with? the man asked.
I have this letter for you, said the messenger.
Good news I hope.
It's a letter about your home, I'm afraid it's not looking good.

Wind howled through the small cracks in the clashing aluminum roof. On the ground, the body of a fat man on his side. Blood pooled around his button-up white collar. Black suit pants and wing-tipped shoes, caked in mud. His lips were open, the bottom one split. A clump of gray hair had fallen across his bruised and plump face. A puncture passing through the nape and a small hole protruding from the Adam's apple, skin flapped outwards like a blooming verbena.

The man motioned. Join me in the barn. I want you to see things how I see 'em. He looked back at his wife, who sat in front of the piano and gave her a short smile. He seemed uneasy.
They walked across the desert lot, a horse neighed from the pasture, and they entered the barn.

The man crouched down over the body and looked up at the woman. She was straight faced – quiet. She pulled her hood back revealing her lightly-freckled face seeming to absorb a stream of light from a hole in the roof. He pointed at the feet of the body. She nodded, walked over and grabbed hold of both legs.

They lifted, the man grasping around the torso. The ass dragged on the ground, their forearms tense. She stepped over the steel framing of the stall, tripping but catching herself. The man let go of the body outside of the stall and opened the sliding door to the outside, illuminating the soiled floor.

They were in the barn. The man leaned next to the lines on the wall.

It's out of my control, said the messenger. You'll need to talk to the bank.

You can't do this to us. We work hard just like anybody else. Give us some time.

Sunlight was blinding. They each pulled at a leg, he on the left, she on the right. Blood trailed on the sand between the arms that dragged and jiggled above the bouncing head. His eyes were fixed on the body. Hers kept focused on the pasture gate ahead, the wind blasting them with sand. An aluminum shingle blew off the shelter roof.

There's nothing I can do. I'm just the messenger.
The man walked over to the hay bales.
Nothing?
It's your problem, call the bank.
Bullshit! said the man. He picked up the hay hook.

It was uphill to the pasture. Russian thistle tumbled past them and dust danced across the surface of the ground like trails of mist. A foxhound barking in the distance towards the snow-capped mountains. Clouds encircled the peaks, coiling from the wind.

Her eyes drifted to the mountains. She thought about the brewing storm. She thought about how this was changing their lives. She drifted into a childhood memory where the rain kept her home, warm next to the fireplace in the arms of her mother. She thought about the law. She thought about God and whether or not she could explain.

~

She walked up the porch steps and crawled into her grandmother's lap and listened. The old woman's voice was shaky and dry. She told the story.

Snowfall had started to stick to the ground as the mounted troops rode in. The river flowing nearby. The natives sat huddled together in blankets trying to stay warm. They had a horseshoe of wagons without horses. A campfire in the center dwindled from the wind and lack of dry wood.

The troops were there to police – to civilize. The savages needed to be taught a lesson about who owned the land. Men, women and children sat staring into the dying campfire, shivering.

You need to leave, said the commander from atop his appaloosa. This is our land now. You have reservations, and we have given you food and shelter. Now, go. Take what we give you.

They did not respond. The cold was overwhelming but the sound of the riverflow gave them comfort. An infant clinging to his mother's neck, his older sister sniffling from the frigid air.

Can you not understand me? said the commander. We have taught you English. This is our land now. You need to leave.

A soldier behind him shifted in his saddle, his finger on the trigger of his Winchester that sat on the saddlehorn and pointed downwards.

We will not leave, said a teenage native who stood up. He had a snaggletooth that could not hide behind his bottom lip. You come here and make us leave, we will not. This is our home. Our land. He turned his back towards the commander and looked towards the river. Blades of grass still blowing in the wind as snow piled around their sheaths.

The commander drew his revolver from its holster and aimed it at the young native.

The gunfire unleashed as the natives tried to flee. Many catching bullets to the back and legs. A small girl ducked under a wagon, shivering.

She watched through the wagonwheel as her family members and friends were massacred.

The firing ceased at the commander's yell.

Get back to camp, he said. Tomorrow, we bury them.

The small girl stared into the campfire and stopped shivering.

~

How about you go back to your bank, and tell 'em we ain't leavin', said the man.

Just take the letter. There's nothing I can do. Please put the hook down.

The man leaned into the handle of the sliding barn door, slamming it shut.

The rain was coming, and the wind was building. The woman continued to pull at the feet of the fat messenger.

The man kept his eyes on the body as they heaved at the legs. He pulled at the muddy shoe. It slipped off and the man fell. The woman stopped and helped him up and he tried to brush the dust off the back of his jeans but quickly gave up. Then they continued, leaving the dead man's shoe lonesome on the desert ground.

He glanced over to her. She sniffled from the cold and wiped her nose across her sleeve.

Their arms ached and the body seemed heavier every inch they dragged as soil built up under the body and into the shirt, adding to the burden. Sand stung their hands and the wind jerked at their clothes and nature itself seemed to be against them.

The man let go of the body and unhooked the lock, opened the chainlink gate and peered out into the grassless pasture. A black-and-white paint running along the far fence chased a neighbor's terrier. The sun above the cloudy mountain peaks in the distance. It was downhill to where a grave roughly larger than the fat man had been dug. And waited. The woman had her back to the pasture, away from the body and the man. He walked over and touched her arm and nodded. She bowed her head slowly and stepped back near the body and they dragged downhill.

Please, don't do this. I didn't do a thing, said the messenger holding his chubby fingers up.

There's nothing I can do, said the man. How about you pay for this?

It relieved them from the uphill grind, but the sand was

softer. Their arms shook and their knees burned, and their backs ached from the weight.

They hauled the body next to the grave and dropped the legs. They both breathed a sigh.

The wind howled across the field. A pile of soil next to the grave slowly diminished into the air at its peak.

He grabbed a rag off the ground and wiped the hay hook clean, then placed it back on the bales. He looked down at the body.

You should have just listened to me. None of this would have happened if you just listened to me.

The man rolled up the sleeves of his sweater and kicked the body by its shoulder into the grave. It was shallow. They looked down at the body, as if praying for a few moments before the man picked up the rusting shovel next to the mound.

The man finished digging the grave and walked back to the house.

He called to his wife, I need your help. I had no choice, he said.

What happened? she asked. His clothes were covered in earth and blood.

Just follow me.

She lifted her head towards the mountains and watched the storm in the distance. It seemed to swirl around the mountaintops. The clouds darkened as the sun descended to the peaks.

The spade scraped through the earth and he lifted the first shovelful. Dust shot up in spirals down the field, the grains of sand too light to stay on the shovel in the high winds. He tried again. A burst of wind caught the soil, spreading it across the pasture ground.

Why are your hands bloody? What did you do?
Please don't ask questions. There's nothing I can do. Turn on the water. He pointed towards the spigot.

He pushed behind the mound with the shovel. The weight was overbearing and his legs shook. Splinters from the shaft of the shovel burrowed into his hands. He stopped and let the shovel fall to the ground. The wind wrenched against their bodies.

He dropped to his knees and tried to push the soil into the grave with his hands. The woman came up behind him, grabbing his shoulders. He stopped.

We can't hide this, she said. We can't.

Biographical Notes & Publication Acknowledgments

Larry Eby writes from the Inland Empire of Southern California. He recently graduated from CSUSB's undergraduate writing program, where he edited the school's literary journal, the *Pacific Review*. Among other magazines, his work has appeared in *Badlands*, the *Sand Canyon Review*, *Welter*, and the *Secret Handshake*. Writer's Digest has awarded his fiction in the top ten of their 79th annual competition. Larry is the co-founder of PoetrIE, an Inland Empire poetry society which holds weekly workshops and readings.

Rivka Keren (born as Katalin Friedländer in Debrecen, Hungary, July 24, 1946) is an Israeli writer. She immigrated to Israel in 1957 and studied painting, philosophy, literature and clinical psychology. So far, she published fifteen books for adults, adolescents and children, won numerous literary prizes and has been translated to English, German, Spanish, Russian, Hungarian and Braille. Her novels, stories and poems are a study of human nature, the destructiveness of evil and revenge, and the power of hope and love. Recently, she recorded an album with the Italian singer and composer Mario Scapecchi and started working with him on a musical. Rivka Keren resides in Gainesville, Florida, and she is married with two children. For further information, please go to: en.wikipedia.org/wiki/Rivka_Keren

Stephen Poleskie is an artist and writer. His artworks are in the collections of numerous museums, and his writing, fiction, and art criticism has appeared in many journals both here and abroad. His work in the anthology *The Book of Love* has been nominated for a Pushcart Prize. He has received grants from the Best Foundation and the New York State Council for the Arts. Currently a professor emeritus at Cornell University, Poleskie lives in Ithaca, N.Y. website: www.StephenPoleskie.com

Arthur Powers went to Brazil with the Peace Corps in 1969 and has lived most his adult life there. From 1985 to 1992 he and his wife worked with subsistence farmers in the Amazon, organizing farmers' unions in a region of violent land conflicts. "Two Foxes" appeared in *XNK*, a magazine in North Carolina. Honors and awards include: Massachusetts Artists Foundation Fellowship in Fiction (1984). Catholic Press Association – annual award for short fiction, 1st place (1995), 2nd place (1998), 3rd place (2006). Tom Howard Fiction Contest, 2nd place (2008), Honorable Mention (2008). Press 53 Open Awards – Finalist (2011). North Carolina State Fiction Contest – Semi-Finalist (2011). Featured Author – *Dappled Things* (9/06). Selected for commemorative anthologies *Sky Songs II* (2005) – best work from *Dreams & Visions*; *Dappled Things* 5th Anniversary Issue (2011). Pushcart Prize nomination (2011).

Lisa M. Sita is a writer and educator whose short stories are heavily influenced by her background in anthropology and history. She has worked professionally as a curriculum developer and instructor while on staff at the American Museum of Natural History, the New-York Historical Society, and the LaGuardia and Wagner Archives, and is the author of several nonfiction books for the school and library market on topics ranging from human evolution, biology and culture, to the lives of American historical figures. She currently works as an assistant director in higher education while continuing to pursue her creative writing.

Patty Somlo has twice been nominated for the Pushcart Prize. Her work has appeared in the *Los Angeles Review*, the *Santa Clara Review*, the *Jackson Hole Review*, and *Fringe Magazine*, and in several anthologies. She lives in Portland, Oregon. Her collection, *From Here to There and Other Stories*, was published in 2010 by Paraguas Books: www.paraguasbooks.com

Janyce Stefan-Cole writes fiction, essay and freelance journalism, and is the author of the novel, *Hollywood Boulevard* (Unbridled Books). A finalist for the James Jones First Novel Fellowship, she is included in the Boston Globe bestselling anthology, *Dick for a Day* (Villard Books), and in *The Healing Muse* and *Knock*

Literary Arts Magazine. A fellow at the Virginia Center for the Creative Arts, she also attended the Squaw Valley Community of Writers, and resides with her husband in Brooklyn, N.Y. and Freedom, N.H. "Conversation with a Tree" was first published in *Knock Literary Arts Magazine*, issue 6.

Andrea Vojtko lives in Arlington, Virginia and is a member of The Writer's Center in Bethesda, Maryland. Her fiction has appeared in the *Potomac Review, Words of Wisdom* and *Road and Travel.* Andrea's story, "Jubilant Voices," in *Words of Wisdom*, was nominated for a 2003 Pushcart prize. She is an avid birder, painter and genealogist.

Kelly Wantuch is a writer and an artist residing in South Bend, Indiana. Her non-fiction essay, "I Shouldn't Have Googled That" (published here as "White Kaleidoscope") won first place in the 2010 English Writing Awards in honor of Lester M. Wolfson at Indiana University South Bend. Kelly has poems, artwork and non-fiction appearing in *Analecta* (2010), *New Views of Gender* (2010), *Preface, Brilliance Bureau* (2011), and *South Bend Museum of Art* (2010 and 2011).

Anne Whitehouse is the author of poetry collections – *The Surveyor's Hand, Blessings and Curses, Bear in Mind,* and *One Sunday Morning* – and the novel, *Fall Love.* Her poems, "Rose's Dream" and "After the Accident" were published in Editions Bibliotekos' *Pain and Memory.* "The Son's Complaint" originally appeared in *The American Voice*, Louisville, Kentucky, No. 16, Fall 1989.

Jeff Vande Zande teaches English at Delta College and writes poetry, fiction, and screenplays. Vande Zande's books of fiction include *Emergency Stopping and Other Stories* (Bottom Dog Press), the novel *Into the Desperate Country* (March Street Press), the novel *Landscape with Fragmented Figures* (Bottom Dog Press) and, most recently, *Threatened Species and Other Stories* (Whistling Shade Press). "Writing on the Wall" originally appeared in *Fifth Wednesday Journal* and then later in, *Threatened Species and Other*

Stories. Jeff's poetry has been nominated for a Pushcart Prize (twice), and one of his poems was selected by Poet Laureate Ted Kooser to appear in his syndicated newspaper column, American Life in Poetry.

James K. Zimmerman is the winner of the 2009 Daniel Varoujan Award and the 2009 & 2010 Hart Crane Memorial Poetry Awards. His work appears or is forthcoming in a*nderbo.com*, *The Bellingham Review, Rosebud, Inkwell, Nimrod, Passager*, and *Vallum*, among others. He is also currently a clinical psychologist in private practice, and was a singer/songwriter in a previous life.

—

One cannot alter one's own peculiar individuality, one's moral character, one's intellectual capacity, one's temperament or physique; and if we go so far as to condemn someone from every point of view, there will be nothing left but to engage us in deadly conflict; for we are practically allowing him or her the right to exist only on condition of becoming another person – which is impossible; nature forbids it.

– Schopenhauer

—

ABOUT EDITIONS BIBLIOTEKOS

Mission and Goals: To produce books of literary merit that address important issues, complex ideas, and enduring themes. We believe in the lasting power of the written word, especially in book form. We believe in contributing to a deeper understanding of what it means to be human (individually and socially) – who we are and what we should do.

For a petit publisher, creating collections is a time-consuming and tedious process, but well worth the effort in producing books worth reading and studying for years to come. Was it in our destiny to become publishers? We are students of philosophy, literature, and history (including interest in science as it relates to human behavior – evolutionary biology, neuroscience, and psychology). We are scholars, academics, and writers – humanists. We are not business people, but somewhere in our intellectual journey we felt more acutely than usual the joy and pain associated with writing and publishing and then made the decision to shepherd other people's work into print.

If you like this book, read (also by Bibliotekos), *Pain and Memory: Reflections on the Strength of the Human Spirit in Suffering* (2009); *Common Boundary: Stories of Immigration* (2010); *Battle Runes: Writings on War* (2011).

www.ebibliotekos.com

Made in the USA
Middletown, DE
10 June 2017